SORAYA NICHOLAS

STARLIGHT
Stables

GYMKHANA HIJINKS

PUFFIN BOOKS

PUFFIN BOOKS

UK | USA | Canada | Ireland | Australia
India | New Zealand | South Africa | China

Penguin Books is part of the Penguin Random House group of companies
whose addresses can be found at global.penguinrandomhouse.com.

Penguin
Random House
Australia

First published by Penguin Random House Australia Pty Ltd, 2016.

Design by Marina Messiha © Penguin Random House Australia Pty Ltd
Cover photography © Caitlin Maloney, Ragamuffin Pet Photography
Printed and bound in Australia by Griffin Press, an accredited ISO AS/NZS 14001
Environmental Management Systems printer.

National Library of Australia Cataloguing-in-Publication data:

Nicholas, Soraya, author.
Starlight stables: gymkhana hijinks / Soraya Nicholas.

978 0 1433 0863 8 (paperback)

For children.
Ponies--Juvenile fiction.
Horse shows--Juvenile fiction.
Friendship--Juvenile fiction.

A823.4

puffin.com.au

PUFFIN BOOKS

STARLIGHT
Stables

GYMKHANA HIJINKS

I'm so lucky to have four fabulous nieces!
For Gabriella, Francesca, Isabella and Genevieve.
I love you all very much.

CHAPTER ONE

Back at Starlight

'Poppy!' An excited scream rang out through the stables. 'You're here!'

Poppy laughed and dropped her bag as she stepped out of the car, spying Milly running full-steam toward her from the other end of the stable block, her dark curls loose and flying out behind her. Poppy ran toward her friend, giggling as her aunt's big dog, Casper, jumped up from his snooze on the hay and bounded alongside her, thinking it was a race.

'You're crazy!' Poppy laughed when Milly almost knocked her over, flinging her arms around her and holding on tight.

It felt good to be back, even if it had only been

1

five days since she'd last been at Starlight Stables.

'Have you seen Joe yet?' Poppy asked, looking past Milly to the stables, hoping for a glimpse of their horses. She still couldn't believe that her aunt and uncle had given her her very own pony. And that it was only three weeks ago that Aunt Sophie and Uncle Mark had brought in Milly and Katie as part of a new scholarship programme, giving Poppy two new horse-crazy friends on the farm. She bet Milly had been straight down to see her horse.

'Are you kidding? Of course!' Milly exclaimed. 'Come on!' She grabbed Poppy's hand and tugged her hard, dragging her toward the stables. Casper trotted along beside them, tongue lolling out and clearly happy to see the girls again.

Poppy pulled back, trying to escape Milly's hold and failing. She was dying to see her pony, but the conversation she'd been having in the car with Aunt Sophie was still playing through her head. She realised she hadn't told Sophie how much it had meant to her, having her at home. In just one week, Sophie had put plans in place so that Poppy didn't have to do all the adult things any more – she'd hired a cleaner, arranged for Poppy's younger brother, Tom, to spend time at different friends' houses over the holidays, and, most importantly of all, she'd got her mum the help she needed.

'Aunt Sophie...' Poppy started, turning to find her aunt at the door to the stables.

'Go,' Aunt Sophie said, waving them away. 'Have fun with your ponies, and come back to the house before six.'

Poppy grinned back at her aunt, who somehow looked immaculate even after their long drive, in a pink shirt and jeans with her blonde hair loose and free.

Aunt Sophie smiled, and Poppy hoped she knew what she'd been trying to say. 'Thank you' hung on her lips, but it just didn't cut it, it didn't say enough.

Poppy's mum hadn't been the same since Poppy's dad had died. But after seeing her mum this week, Poppy felt that everything was starting to feel better now. Her mum seemed happy about being in therapy, and so it had been worth telling her aunt how tough things had been at home. And, with Tom staying at friends' houses, Poppy didn't feel so terrible about leaving her little brother behind while she came back to Starlight.

Poppy ran as fast as she could alongside Milly, boots skidding on the concrete floor outside the tack room. Her heart was pounding and she was panting when they stopped.

'Do you think we should wait for Katie?' asked Poppy. She knew Katie would be here soon, and that she'd be desperate to see her pony, Cody.

'No way,' Milly said, not slowing down. She disappeared into the tack room and came back out with both their halters. 'I'm not waiting another second to bring Joe in.'

Poppy shrugged and took her halter and lead rope from Milly, slinging it over her shoulder. She didn't want to wait, either – it felt like forever since she'd seen Crystal. They walked past all the looseboxes, stopping only to pat Sophie's horse, Jupiter. The smell of horse made Poppy smile – that mixture of sawdust, manure, horse sweat and hard feed was heaven to her.

'Wait up!'

Poppy and Milly spun round at the same time, laughing when they almost knocked each other over.

'Katie!' Poppy squealed, running toward her friend and elbowing Milly out of the way to hug her first. They ended up in a tangle of arms, all giggling.

They'd only known each other a couple of weeks, but Poppy already thought of them as her best friends.

'It feels like we've been away forever,' Katie said with a sigh.

'I know,' Milly replied. 'I was so worried my parents weren't going to let me come back.'

After what they'd been through the last time they were together, trying to rescue stolen horses from a scary neighbour's farm, Poppy had worried the same thing. She felt for the hair tie around her wrist and dropped her halter, scooping her long brown hair up into a ponytail so it was off her face.

'My stupid mum thinks I should be doing a summer school programme instead of riding. You know, to make sure I'm *ah-mazing* at maths,' Milly continued, rolling her eyes.

Poppy slung an arm around Milly's shoulder, realising just how much she had missed her friends. She was as excited about being back with Milly and Katie as she was about seeing Crystal. She couldn't imagine holidays here without them now.

'Would a bareback race make you feel better?' Poppy asked.

Milly's smile lit her whole face. 'Halters only?

Race up from the paddock?'

Poppy watched Katie race off to grab her halter and then skid back to a stop beside them, linking arms with Poppy. Poppy linked her other arm through Milly's, and they walked down to the paddock, chatting about how much they'd missed their ponies.

And then she saw her. Poppy let go of her friends' arms and stood still, watching as Crystal's head rose, still munching grass as she stared straight back at her. It was like Poppy was in a bubble; she didn't know what else was going on around her, couldn't focus on anything except her pony grazing at the other end of the paddock. It still seemed like a dream, the fact that she had her own horse. When Aunt Sophie and Uncle Mark had given Crystal to her when she'd arrived for the Christmas holidays, it had been the best thing that had ever happened in her life. And now Poppy was back again, and she had two whole weeks of riding Crystal before she had to go home for the start of a new school year.

'Crystal,' she called. 'Hey, girl.'

Poppy kept her halter over her shoulder and walked though the gate, over to Crystal, hoping the pony wouldn't trot off. She was desperate to race over

but she knew how to approach a horse properly –
slowly and confidently. She reached into her pocket
and took out a sugar cube, holding it flat in her palm
as she walked. An excited tingle went up Poppy's
spine as Crystal stretched her neck out. Poppy felt
Crystal's breath hot on her skin as the pony nuzzled
the sugar from her hand, warm brown eyes focused
on hers.

Poppy slipped the halter over Crystal's nose,
then worked the other part over the back of her ears
and clasped it. Once she had it secure, she held the
rope in one hand and threw her other arm around
Crystal's neck, breathing in the sweet smell of her,
loving the softness of her horse's coat on her cheek.

'Hurry up, slow coach!' Milly called out.

Poppy looked over her shoulder and saw that
Milly and Katie were already sitting astride their
ponies, waiting for her.

'Just a sec,' she called back, clipping her lead rope
on to one side of Crystal's halter, and then moving
around to tie the end of the rope to the other side.
She put her makeshift reins over Crystal's head,
then vaulted onto her back, holding a big tuft of her
mane, the other hand flat on her back to help propel

her body up. She landed a bit wobbly, but she was up, and Poppy slung her arms around Crystal's neck for a quick cuddle before they moved.

'Last one back to the stables…'

Poppy burst out laughing and pressed her legs to Crystal's side, trotting then cantering off before Milly even had a chance to issue her orders. Crystal was fast, and Poppy was only just staying on, her horse's coat slippery against her jods as she dug her knees in and held tighter to Crystal's mane, trying not to fall.

'You're a cheat, Poppy!' Milly yelled from behind.

Poppy knew that Katie was hot on her heels, but she leaned closer to Crystal, flat to her neck, and urged her to go faster. They weren't cantering that fast, but with no saddle it felt like a gallop. Jods were always super slippery, and she noticed that her friends had worn theirs up in the car, too, and so knew they'd be holding on as tightly as she was.

'Aaaargh!!'

Poppy sat up straighter and looked over her shoulder just in time to see Milly flying through the air. Poppy tugged hard to get Crystal to stop, pulling on the lead rope and managing to turn her around. She clamped her hand over her mouth, trying not to laugh, but it was impossible; Joe was standing with his nostrils flared, looking down at Milly as she sat on the ground.

'Don't you dare laugh at me,' Milly said.

Poppy looked at Katie and couldn't hold it in any longer – she and Katie laughed so hard that tears ran down Poppy's cheeks.

When she finally stopped laughing, her cheeks hurt and she had the hiccups.

'That was so not funny,' Milly said, hands on her hips as she glared at her pony. Joe had always been the rascally one, more unpredictable than the others. 'He just bucked and, bam, I went flying!'

'We know, we saw!' Katie said, and then she gave Poppy a look that made them both burst into giggles again.

Milly made to take Joe's lead rope, but he danced sideways and trotted off. Through watery eyes from laughing so hard, Poppy saw Milly march after him, but he kept sidestepping, staying just out of her reach before cantering off to the other side of the paddock.

'Joe!' yelled Milly. 'Get back here.'

Poppy and Katie rode their horses over to Milly, halting on either side of her.

'You do know that this makes you the loser, right?' Poppy said.

'Ha ha, yes, I know.'

'So that means you have to do our chores,' Katie continued, grinning at Poppy over Milly's head.

'Fine, whatever,' Milly muttered, brushing the mud off her jods, the dirt on her face making her freckles look like they were all joined together.

Poppy decided not to tell her about the grass stains on her bottom from where she'd landed. She knew Milly only had one pair of cream jods and that she'd hate knowing they were all mucky already.

'Come on, hop up behind me,' Poppy said, holding out her hand.

Milly sighed, turning and putting her hands on Crystal's bottom instead of taking Poppy's hand, and vaulting up behind Poppy. Poppy felt Milly's arms wrap around her waist.

'He hates me,' Milly mumbled. 'I can't believe he did that.'

'He doesn't hate you,' Poppy told her, squeezing

her legs against Crystal's side and directing her over to Joe. 'He's just having too good a time eating all this grass.'

She exchanged glances with Katie and they both rode over. Katie was ahead, and Poppy couldn't help but admire her perfectly clean jods and her perfectly plaited blonde hair that hung in a straight line down her back. Katie always looked so neat and tidy – unlike Milly, Poppy thought to herself with a chuckle, whose curls were as unruly as she was.

'I'll grab Joe's rope, and Katie, you stay close behind him while Milly tries to mount him,' Poppy ordered. She knew that Joe was less likely to move away with his horse friends so close.

Poppy reached over and grabbed Joe's rope and felt Milly slither down off Crystal behind her. Milly quietly took hold, jumped up and was mounted.

As Crystal moved away, Poppy heard Milly warn Joe, 'Do that again and I'll give Crystal all the carrots I've been saving for you.' Poppy was sure Joe huffed in response.

They all turned around and headed back in the direction of the stables, the three of them riding side by side.

'Want to trot?' Poppy asked.

The other two nodded and they bounced along, all holding on with their legs and clasping handfuls of mane, trying not to fall off.

'Hey, isn't that the mean girl from the practice gymkhana?' Katie asked.

They slowed back to a walk and watched as a girl with a thick and long dark braid unloaded a perfect-looking bay pony from a shiny black horse float. It was being towed by a smart-looking Range Rover, and it made Poppy sigh; she'd do anything for her mum to have a four-wheel drive to pull a float like that.

'It *is* her,' Katie said. 'I'd never forget that horse.'

The girl held the end of her horse's rope and looked around. Poppy couldn't see clearly from where they were at the edge of the paddocks, but she thought the girl looked like she had her nose stuck up in the air.

As Poppy, Milly and Katie rode closer, Poppy noticed that the pony was wearing blue floating boots that fully covered her lower legs, and a handsome blue-and-red rug with tiny holes all over so it wasn't too hot for her. The girl stared at them, her gaze cold as ice. Poppy remembered seeing her, recalled the glare she'd given Katie when she'd done well in the jumping round. She knew Katie was right; it was definitely her.

'I'd never forget that smug look on her face, like she's a million times better than us,' Milly whispered.

Poppy stopped looking at the girl. 'She's not better than us,' she said. 'She hates us because Katie won against her that day. I remember her, too.'

'So what's she doing here?' Katie asked.

'Beats me, but my guess is that she's probably taking lessons here now,' Poppy said.

She was used to seeing all types of riders coming to visit her aunt for lessons, and Poppy had learned not to be bothered by them. But she was with her friends on this one; there was something unsettling about this girl, and Poppy certainly wasn't pleased to see her here when she'd been so frosty with them all at the gymkhana. But curiosity had the better of her, and she was dying to get a closer look at the girl and her pony.

CHAPTER TWO

Jessica

They jumped off their ponies when they reached the stables, feet thudding down onto the hard packed dirt. Poppy had steered them all straight into the stables rather than riding around and past where the mean girl was – it would be easier to investigate without their ponies.

January was hot, and everything was getting so dry already. Poppy bet they'd see a lot more kangaroos around the farm now that there was less water around elsewhere. Every summer, animals tucked themselves into the shade of the massive blue gum and oak trees that were in every paddock.

'If Mrs D asks us to show that girl around, I'll

die,' Milly muttered dramatically, calling Poppy's aunt by the name she'd come up with when she and Katie had first arrived. Poppy liked that her friends had clicked with Aunt Sophie, and fallen into an easy way with her from the get-go.

Poppy laughed as they walked the ponies into the stables. 'You're such a drama queen.'

Milly made a face and poked her tongue out just as the mean girl walked around the corner, heading straight for them. Poppy's laughter died in her throat, and she gently tugged on Crystal's rope to make her stop. Her pony's head was over her shoulder as she stood beside her, and Poppy reached up to stroke her muzzle.

They all stood there, staring. No one said a word to the girl who was glaring at them. They'd only seen her once before, but there was something about her Poppy didn't like – and it was pretty obvious her friends thought the same. The girl didn't have her horse with her. Poppy guessed she'd tied her up to the side of the float.

'Um, hi,' Poppy managed, amazed that even saying hello felt like a struggle.

Aunt Sophie rounded the corner and almost

banged straight into the mean girl. 'Girls, there you are! I want you all to meet Jessica.'

Poppy gripped the rope tighter. She was pretty sure this girl was here for private lessons, and she knew how important that made her for Sophie, who relied on the money from private lessons to keep the farm going. And so Poppy forced a smile.

'I'm Poppy,' she said through her fake smile. 'And this is Katie and Milly.'

Poppy watched as Katie waved, and she glared at Milly until Milly unwrinkled her nose and smiled, too. Poppy was about to ask Jessica what her horse's name was, but the girl never said a word, just tapped her riding crop against her boot and stared off into the distance. Up close, her dark hair was crazy-shiny, and it was so immaculately swept back into a plait that Poppy couldn't imagine her wearing a helmet.

'I'm just about to show Jessica around the stables and arena,' Aunt Sophie continued.

Maybe she hadn't noticed how rude her new pupil was being, Poppy thought, or maybe she was just trying not to make a big deal about it.

'She's going to be training here for a little while,

and depending on how she likes it she might be keeping her horse here next week, leading up to the Pony Club Gymkhana.' Aunt Sophie laughed. 'Heck, if she likes it that much she might decide to stay here herself, like Milly and Katie.'

Stay? This Jessica couldn't stay. No way. It would ruin everything.

Her face must have betrayed some of what she was thinking, because Aunt Sophie gave her a quizzical look before steering Jessica out of the stables.

'Is it okay if we go for a trail ride?' Poppy asked her aunt before she walked off.

'Of course. Just remember that the horses might all be a bit frisky after not being ridden for a week.'

'Did you see Joe buck Milly off?' Katie asked, clamping her hand over her mouth when she started to laugh.

'Oh, Milly, are you okay?' Aunt Sophie asked, eyebrows raised and her mouth twisted up into a smile, like she was trying not to laugh, too. 'What happened?'

'I'm fine. Just angry with him,' Milly said with a huff.

'Cleopatra would never buck,' Jessica said, still

looking bored. 'And she would hate going on a trail ride.'

The girls stayed silent, all staring at Aunt Sophie and hoping she would say something. If Poppy's mum ever heard her speak like that she'd be in so much trouble, but Aunt Sophie just gave them a smile and touched her hand to Jessica's back, guiding her away.

'It's very important not to ride your horse in an arena every day,' Poppy heard Sophie say. 'Horses need a combination of workouts for their muscle development, and, more importantly, to keep their minds fresh.'

'My old instructor was perfectly happy for me to train in the arena every day. That's what I like doing,' Jessica insisted.

'I don't want you doing anything you don't like here, Jessica, but I have you and your horse's best interests at heart.'

'Cleopatra would never buck,' Milly mimicked as soon as Sophie and Jessica were out of earshot.

'I don't like her,' Katie said, leading Cody to his stall.

'I can't believe she's going to be here every day,'

Poppy moaned, following Katie's lead and taking Crystal to her stall. 'And we have to be *nice* to her.'

'No, we don't,' Milly said, closing the door to Joe's stall once he was inside, and marching down toward the tack room.

'We do,' Poppy said firmly. 'It doesn't matter if we like her or not – we have to be the nice ones.'

'She's here. And she's gorgeous.' Katie had walked past the tack room and kept going, and when Poppy poked her head out to see what she was talking about, she saw her staring into one of the looseboxes.

Poppy and Milly hurried over and stood next to Katie, all three staring at the new horse. The mare *was* gorgeous, there was no other way to describe her. Poppy felt mean thinking about how beautiful this horse was when she loved Crystal so much, but Cleopatra looked like she should be in a magazine. Her rug had been removed, and her dark bay coat was shiny and slightly dappled over her flank, with black legs even more glossy than the rest of her. She was the kind of pony Poppy had always wished for and known she would never in her life be able to afford. Jessica must have brought her in while they were mucking around in the paddock still.

'Poor horse, having *Jessica* as her rider,' Milly said, stepping forward and holding out her hand to her.

The horse stopped munching on her hay and came closer, nuzzling Milly's hand, ears pricked forward.

'At least we know she's nothing like her rider.' Poppy slipped one of the sugar cubes from her pocket and let her have it, feeling sorry for her. 'I bet Jessica's mean to her. And she's so sweet!'

She watched as Katie blew on the horse's nose, tickling under her chin and then starting to scratch her. Cleopatra rubbed her lips roughly over Katie's shoulder in return, scratching her back and making them all laugh.

'What are you doing?'

Poppy froze, and her friends did, too. When she was finally brave enough to turn around, Poppy saw Jessica standing there, hands on her hips, riding crop still dangling from one hand.

'We were just saying hello,' Poppy said. 'She's beautiful.'

Jessica looked grumpy, her dark eyes narrowed.

'Well she's mine, and I don't want anyone touching her except me.'

Her friends backed away, but Poppy gave the mare one last defiant pat and whispered 'sorry' in the horse's ear. Then they all walked off and disappeared into the tack room. Milly shut the door behind them and they huddled together, heads bent.

'We have to tell Mrs D what she's really like,' Katie said.

'I think she already knows,' Poppy replied. 'But Jessica's probably paying so much for lessons that she doesn't want to turn her away. And besides, just because she's not nice doesn't mean she doesn't deserve to ride here. Sophie's a great teacher, and Jessica probably loves horses as much as we do.' She didn't like it any more than the others, but what could they do?

Milly grabbed a bag she must have stashed by her saddle earlier and came back with three Freddo Frogs. Poppy grinned as she took one, peeling off the wrapper straightaway and taking a bite of the chocolate. These strawberry-filled ones were her favourite.

'At least she doesn't like trail riding, so she's not

going to want to tag along with us,' Poppy pointed out.

'I think we should just act normal, and let Mrs D see for herself how mean she really is,' Katie said. 'We can't get into any trouble, not again – Mrs D wouldn't have any choice but to send us home, especially after last time – so we need to be the good ones.'

'Agreed,' Poppy said. 'We just need to ignore Jessica and have fun riding. We might not even have to see her much.'

Poppy bet they'd actually be seeing a whole lot of her, but she wasn't going to tell the others that. Maybe she could ask Aunt Sophie about Jessica later, without Katie and Milly around, to see what she really thought about her new pupil.

'Well, *I'm* not speaking to her, I'm not riding with her, and I'm not…' Milly's voice cut off.

'Girls, why is the door shut?' Aunt Sophie walked in with Jessica right behind her.

Poppy just about jumped out of her skin she got such a fright. She swallowed the rest of the Freddo she'd stuffed into her mouth.

'Um, we thought we saw a mouse,' Milly said,

smiling sweetly. 'We wanted to catch it instead of letting it run out.'

Aunt Sophie raised her eyebrows, like she wasn't sure whether to believe Milly or not.

'Jessica, do you want to help us catch it?' Milly asked.

Poppy tried her hardest to hide a smile when Jessica looked horrified. Jessica was already backing out of the room, shaking her head.

'They're just harmless, cute little things,' Poppy added, even though she actually hated mice.

'Milly's just teasing you, aren't you Milly?' Aunt Sophie said, staring at Milly like she was waiting for her to nod. 'Our stable cat makes quick work of any field mice, and I haven't seen one for a very long time.'

Jessica didn't look convinced, but Milly looked happy with herself as she lifted her saddle up and let it rest on her hip.

Poppy had a feeling that things were going to go from bad to worse with Jessica, and her bold and teasing friend was definitely going to be the cause of it. Just like last time.

CHAPTER THREE

Fun with Friends

Poppy, Milly and Katie sat around the table with Sophie and Mark, eating Uncle Mark's famous spaghetti and meatballs. It always made Poppy smile when he announced he'd be cooking, because he only knew how to make one thing so she always knew what to expect. She adored her uncle – he was the local vet and incredible with animals, and one of her favourite things was going along on call-outs with him to see him help sick or injured animals.

'Were all of the ponies well behaved today?' he asked, watching the girls from the other side of the table.

'No!' Milly blurted. 'We were riding bareback

24

and Joe bucked and sent me flying.'

Poppy hid her grin with her hand, remembering how funny it had been seeing the chestnut pony's nostrils flared.

'Land in horse poo?' Uncle Mark asked with a grin.

'No, but I was so angry with him. He's so perfect sometimes, and then he goes and does something like that,' Milly grumbled.

'Hey, if there was no landing in poo it can't have been that bad, right?'

Milly laughed and Poppy joined in. It was what Poppy liked most about her new friend – she was always the first to giggle, even if she was the one being made fun of.

'The girls met Jessica today,' Aunt Sophie told Mark, twirling spaghetti around her fork. 'Poor girl thought there was a mouse in the stables and wouldn't set foot in the tack shed again.'

Uncle Mark's eyebrows shot up. 'And why did she have that idea?'

Poppy stayed silent and so did the others.

'Milly may have played a trick on her,' Aunt Sophie said.

'No, not Milly!' Uncle Mark exclaimed, making them all giggle again.

'She's awful,' Milly said, her eyes wide as she set her fork down. 'She won't talk to us, and she even told us not to touch her horse. Ever.'

Poppy looked at Aunt Sophie and saw her frown.

'She's just different, Milly,' her aunt said. 'You girls get along so well because you're all similar in a way, which is wonderful, but I need you to make an effort with her. It's important to me.'

'But she hates us,' Poppy said, not able to stay quiet any longer. She couldn't see how they'd be able to make an effort with somebody who clearly didn't want anything to do with them. 'I know you need her here, Aunt Sophie, but don't make us spend time with her, please. She was so mean to Katie when she won the show jumping at your gymkhana, and she treats us like we're...'

'What?' Aunt Sophie sounded impatient.

Poppy's cheeks burned hot because she didn't know what to say and she knew how silly it sounded moaning about the new girl.

'She's just not nice,' she eventually mumbled, wishing one of the others would say something now.

She glanced sideways and saw that Milly and Katie were looking down at their plates.

'I'm sure Jessica will warm up,' Uncle Mark said. 'Her mum's pretty annoying, too, so can't say it surprises me.'

'Mark!' Aunt Sophie scolded.

He looked guilty, standing to clear the plates and winking at the girls. Poppy loved that her uncle always kind of understood what she was trying to say and took her side on things. But her aunt was the one in charge when it came to the riding school, and so if she said Jessica was here to stay, then there was nothing anyone could do about it.

'Just give her a chance, girls, that's all I'm asking,' Aunt Sophie said. 'The three of you started out wishing for a pony, and you became great little riders through hard work and perseverance. *Then* you got your horses.' She sighed, making Poppy realise how tired she looked. 'Jessica was given an expensive pony before she could even ride, and her mother has always expected her to be an excellent equestrian simply because the horse beneath her is perfect. Sometimes, appearances can be deceiving, that's all I'm saying.'

'Okay,' Poppy muttered. 'I just wanted to tell you what she was really like.'

'Yeah, sorry, Mrs D. No more pranks,' Milly said.

Poppy started clearing the plates from the table, and Milly and Katie followed her into the kitchen. They rinsed everything and loaded the dishwasher, staying in the kitchen until the job was done before racing up the stairs to the room they all shared.

'You guys should have backed me up,' Poppy hissed. 'It looked like I was the mean one, not her.'

'I didn't know what to say,' Katie said. 'But you're right, we sounded like the mean girls who didn't want to make her feel welcome.'

'We need to wait,' Milly announced, flopping down onto Poppy's bed – the one real bed in the room which they all always sat on together. Poppy pulled the doona up that had been folded at the end of the bed, and they all put their legs under it. It was summer, but there was a chill in the air this evening, and Poppy liked having something to snuggle while they chatted.

'We need to stop moaning and just let Mrs D see the real her,' Milly continued. 'There's no way she can keep being nice in front of her and mean behind her back.'

'But she's not even nice in front of her!' Poppy moaned.

'Milly's right,' Katie agreed. 'We need to either catch her doing something awful so we can tell the Ds about her, or let Mrs D see for herself so that she stops giving her lessons.'

'So what do we do in the meantime?' Poppy asked.

Milly shrugged. 'We be nice to her when we have to, but otherwise we just pretend like she's not even here.'

'Pretend like Miss Fancy Pants isn't here?' Poppy shuddered. 'Impossible.'

She jumped off the bed, feeling irritated, and grabbed her phone from the side table. There was a message from Sarah, and she smiled when she read it. Sarah was her best friend back home, and Poppy always missed her so much when she came here, even when she was busy with horse things.

'My friend Sarah's so bored at home,' Poppy told the others, reading her message.

'She should come here. Bet I'd like her a whole

lot more than I like *Jessica*.'

Poppy laughed. 'Or not. She's heaps of fun, but she doesn't like horses at all.'

A knock on the door made them all look up.

'Just me,' Uncle Mark called out.

'Come in,' Poppy called back.

Poppy dropped her phone back on the table as the door swung open. Mark came in carrying a tray with three steaming mugs of hot chocolate. They all jumped up when they saw what it was.

'Something nice for your first night back,' he told them, putting the tray down on the bedside table. 'And Casper was looking for you.'

Casper pushed around Mark's legs, his shaggy tail wagging and his tongue hanging out. The Australian shepherd was insanely friendly and always wanted to hang out with the girls. Although he usually spent more time snoring and lying upside down, hoping someone would tickle his belly, than with his ears pricked listening to them.

'Can he sleep in here with us tonight?' Milly asked.

'I think that's exactly what he has in mind,' Uncle Mark said, dropping a hand to the dog's head and giving him a rub. 'Now tell me,' he whispered, dropping onto the edge of the bed. 'Is this girl Jessica really as bad as you say?'

They all huddled closer to Mark. Poppy cradled her mug of hot chocolate, drinking in its warmth. She nodded, and the others did the same.

'She's, like, so mean,' Milly said.

'She just glares at us like she wants to turn us to ice with her stare or something,' Katie added.

Uncle Mark nodded. 'I see.'

'Is there anything you can do about her?' Poppy piped up, hoping he might speak to Sophie for them and give them permission to avoid Jessica.

He shook his head. 'No. But I believe you,' he said. 'And I promise to make you hot chocolates and bring you Tim Tams every night if you girls promise to tell me all the mean things she does and… be nice to her.'

They all groaned.

'Promise me.' he insisted.

'Uncle Mark!' Poppy moaned.

'Sorry, girls, but there's three of you, and one of her. Just stay out of her way and try to have fun.'

He grinned and walked back out, pulling the

door shut behind him.

'At least he believes us,' Poppy said to Milly and Katie, although it did nothing to wipe the disappointed looks from their faces.

They sat and sipped their hot chocolates, and Poppy hoped the next two weeks were going to be as fun as the first. Jessica had put a damper on their first day back, but Poppy was determined not to let her ruin the rest of the holidays. Too soon, she'd be back at school, having to pretend like she cared about maths and english when all she really wanted was to be back here riding. She would enjoy herself now, with or without Jessica, especially as she didn't have the worry of her mum and little brother hanging over her this time.

Poppy's mind flitted to her mum. She wondered how she was finding the retreat Sophie had got her into, and how her therapy sessions were going. When Sophie had gone home with Poppy, she'd made things better straightaway. She'd got her mum into the retreat, where Poppy knew she'd spent a lot of time with a grief counsellor because Poppy had seen the counsellor as well. The counsellor had explained to Poppy what the process was for her mum. It made Poppy feel better, knowing what was going on, and Poppy was amazed how much better her mum seemed even after just a couple of days. It was like someone had flicked a switch, and her mum had come back. Even though her mum was still sad, she was smiling again, and she'd done nothing but hug Poppy the whole time they'd spent together.

Poppy set down her mug and reached for her phone again to send her mum a quick text to say hi. She doubted Milly and Katie or even Sarah could really understand how hard it had been, having her mum be so weird for so long, but that was okay. She didn't need them to understand everything. They'd listened when she'd needed them to, and she knew they would again. And that's all that mattered.

Poppy bounced out of bed in the morning and powered through her vegemite toast before racing to the stables with the others. The horses were stabled at night, so all they had to do was brush them down then saddle up in the mornings. Every second day, they had a lesson scheduled with Aunt Sophie. The other days were free days, so they got to choose where they wanted to ride. But today was a lesson day.

Poppy ran the dandy brush down Crystal's legs, loving every second she got to spend with her. She still couldn't believe that she had her own horse now. Aunt Sophie and Uncle Mark had been so good to her, and it made her feel bad for moaning about Jessica the night before. The girl might be mean, but it wasn't like she was going to ruin their holiday.

Poppy swapped brushes and used a soft body one over Crystal's back, following the grooves of her body. Her coat was fine because it was summer, and small light brown freckles were just visible. Poppy wondered if she'd look almost white over winter when her coat grew thick.

'You ready?' Milly called out.

'Almost,' Poppy called back. She was always in a hurry to get down to the horses, but it was Milly who was impatient to get on horseback all the time. Poppy was happy so long as she was doing something with Crystal.

She slipped Crystal's halter off and brushed her face gently, loving how Crystal closed her eyes and let her cradle her face. She loved that her pony already trusted her so much.

Knowing that Milly would be getting annoyed with her for taking so long, she put on the saddle blanket then saddle, not doing the girth up too tight yet. She took her bridle, slipped her finger into the side of Crystal's lips and carefully put the bit in her mouth, securing the leather behind her ears and doing up first the throat latch and then the nose band. Her fingers worked the leather easily, like second nature to her now. She'd been learning and helping at the riding school for so long that everything about gearing the horses up and being in the saddle felt so natural to her.

The familiar clip-clop of hooves sounded out along the concrete of the stable block at the same time as Poppy was pulling on her leather riding gloves inside Crystal's stall. Aunt Sophie had given them to her when they were back home in Melbourne, while her mum was gone, and Poppy loved the feeling of holding the reins when she was wearing them. They made her feel grown-up, the leather soft against her hands rather than the roughness of the reins. She gave Crystal a quick pat, led her through the stable door and then out into the open, following her friends as they headed toward the mounting block. Milly and Katie mounted first, then Poppy, and they were riding out toward the arena for their morning lesson when Jessica rounded the far corner of the stable building. Poppy noticed her scowl when she saw them.

'Morning,' Poppy called out, forcing a bright smile and silently cursing Milly and Katie who carried on riding past them.

Jessica stared at her. 'Hi.' She was dressed in her riding gear and was wearing the most beautiful long black leather boots. Her mum must have just dropped her off.

At least she'd said something, Poppy thought. Poppy nudged Crystal with her heels and headed off after the others, rolling her shoulders back and sitting as straight as she could. She wanted to make sure Aunt Sophie noticed how much she'd remembered from her last lesson when she saw her.

'Morning again, girls,' Aunt Sophie called out from the arena once they were close, leading her big gelding, Jupiter. He was all sweaty, and Poppy noticed that she'd already loosened off his girth.

He was walking along beside her with his head low, tired but looking happy, and when her aunt stopped he rubbed his head on her shoulder.

'Do you want us to go get warmed up, Mrs D?' Katie asked.

Aunt Sophie nodded, tucking the reins under one arm and removing her black velvet riding helmet. She let her long blonde hair out, put her fingers through it, and then scooped it up into a high ponytail. Poppy was mesmerised by her aunt. She somehow managed to look so glamorous even when just putting her hair up.

'I'm just going to take Jupiter back in and give him a quick brush down, then I'll be ready,' Sophie said. 'You girls get started.'

'Sure thing,' Milly replied for them all.

'Oh, and girls?' Aunt Sophie said, pushing Jupiter back when his head-rubbing became even more vigorous. 'Jessica will be joining you for your lesson this morning. I thought we'd start off with a refresh of everything in the arena, and then move on to some gymkhana training – have some fun with your horses for your first morning back.'

Poppy smiled and hoped her aunt didn't notice

that it was fake. She loved training for games, but the fact that Jessica was joining them kind of took the excitement out of it.

Poppy, Milly and Katie rode off toward the arena, three abreast, not saying anything about Jessica. She bet her friends felt the same way she did.

'I love Jupiter almost as much as I love Cody,' Katie said with a sigh. 'Imagine having a horse like him one day.' Katie bent down and put her arms around Cody's golden neck as they walked. 'Close your ears, Cody.'

'He is amazing,' Poppy agreed. 'Sophie's had him since he was a foal, so he's been with her a long time. It's like he just reads her mind when she asks him to do something.' The big warm blood gelding was 17 hands high, and he was the most graceful, incredible horse Poppy had ever seen.

'Come on, let's start riding before Jessica gets here,' Milly said, gathering up her reins.

Poppy did the same, gathering her reins so she had a gentle contact with Crystal's mouth, and pushing her heels down. Last time they'd been at the farm, Aunt Sophie had told them to ride their horses in the arena more seriously, to ask them to accept the bit and practise as if they were in a competition. Poppy tried doing just that, and was pleased when Crystal did as she was asked, head going down so that her neck was slightly curved.

And then Jessica entered the arena at a trot, flicking her whip against her horse's flank when her poor pony so much as looked at the other horses. Poppy felt herself get wound up as Jessica did it again. She wanted to yell at her and tell her not to hit her horse when the mare was doing nothing wrong, but she bit the soft skin on the inside of her mouth and kept quiet.

Instead, Poppy focused on Crystal, slipping one hand down to stroke her neck, and thinking that maybe Jessica wouldn't be so easy to ignore after all.

CHAPTER FOUR

Lesson Time

'Okay, girls, listen up,' Aunt Sophie called out. 'I have the jumps all set up in an easy course, and I'm going to time you. Since this is practice for the gymkhana, I want you to treat each other as competitors.'

Poppy's heart was racing, excited about jumping and already puffing from the trotting and canter work they'd just finished in the arena. Aunt Sophie had told them that they were going to practise show jumping, then do the bending poles, and Poppy loved both.

'Ride your ponies confidently, look over each jump, not at it, and, most importantly, have fun.'

Poppy shortened her stirrups by two holes on

each side so she'd be able to easily rise out of the saddle for jumping. Crystal patiently stood still for her while she had her legs loose by her sides, but the moment she pushed her boots back into the stirrups and gathered her reins, Crystal started to dance on the spot, eager to get going – she knew exactly what they were about to do.

'Poppy, you go first,' Aunt Sophie called out.

Poppy heard Jessica make a grunting sound, but she ignored her. Her aunt didn't pick favourites, it was only that Poppy had been ready first. So she pressed her legs to Crystal's sides before Jessica made a fuss and insisted on being the first one around the course.

Poppy pushed Crystal into a canter, sitting deep in the saddle and completing a full circle before she rode toward the first jump. She knew her aunt would have started the timer the second she cantered past the flag, but once they cleared the first jump she didn't think of anything other than the feeling of her horse beneath her. Crystal fought to go faster, but Poppy remembered her lessons, sat deeper in the saddle to slow her down to a controllable speed for jumping, legs to her sides and reins firm but not too tight. They approached the second jump and Poppy encouraged Crystal, keeping her eyes raised and looking ahead to the next one, the brightly coloured poles arranged in a criss-cross style. She leaned forward, heels planted down to keep her balance, hands moving up Crystal's neck to release the reins like Aunt Sophie had taught her as they soared through the air. Soon, they were at the last jump, clearing it with ease and racing toward the finish line.

'Well done, Poppy!' Aunt Sophie called out.

Katie and Milly were cheering as she slowed to a walk, then pulled up beside them.

'That was awesome,' Milly said. 'Bet we can't do as well as you.'

Jessica stayed silent, but it didn't worry Poppy. Her friends were proud of her, just like she would be of them if they did a clear round in a good time.

'One minute fifty,' Aunt Sophie said. 'You're up next, Milly.'

Milly trotted off, and Poppy could see that she was having to be firm with Joe. He was headstrong and excited whenever they jumped, and today was no different. But after being cantered in a circle before starting, taking off too early for the first jump and then easily clearing the second, he started to visibly relax. Poppy winced when they knocked a rail on the fifth jump, though, and then the sixth, but he soared over the last two fences, ears pricked even as Milly visibly clamped her legs tight against him, and they raced toward the finish flag.

'Woo hoo!' Poppy cheered, dropping her reins on Crystal's neck and clapping. Her horse was standing still, ears forward but head down and relaxed, neck stretched out. Crystal knew she'd had her turn and she was happy to just stand now.

'You beat Poppy by ten seconds, but the two rails down mean she's still the leader,' Aunt Sophie said. 'Great job, though.'

Milly was grinning ear to ear, and when she passed Jessica she poked out her tongue, which made Poppy laugh even though she knew she shouldn't. Katie was up next, and she soared around the course, nice and steady in a clear round, but she was slower than Poppy. Then it was Jessica's turn.

'Good luck,' Poppy said, forcing a smile.

Jessica just stared at her as she rode past, giving her horse a kick in the sides and a tap with her whip when they entered the ring.

Poppy glanced at Katie and saw that she was frowning. 'I hate that she hits her,' Katie said. 'She's got such a great pony, and she doesn't need to.'

'I know,' Poppy sighed. It wasn't nice but it wasn't technically cruel, either. Plenty of riders used crops, and she knew her aunt would only make a fuss about it if she saw a rider actually hitting their horse hard and often.

Poppy couldn't help admiring Jessica's horse. Cleopatra was stunning when she moved, cantering perfectly toward the first fence and clearing it with ease. She continued faultlessly around the rest of the course, heading toward the final jump, ears pricked as she gracefully covered the ground. They popped over easily, but Jessica had still tapped her with her whip just before take off, which had made the mare hesitate a little, her back leg hanging slightly as she jumped, just knocking the top rail. It wobbled and eventually fell, but Jessica acted like she hadn't even noticed it, racing toward the finish line and throwing her fist in the air like she'd just won the Grand Prix.

'Great round, Jessica!' Aunt Sophie enthused. She held up her stopwatch. 'One minute forty-two.'

Jessica was grinning as she rode toward them. Poppy realised it was the first time she'd actually seen her smile properly.

'Ready to put the jumps up higher?' Jessica asked no one in particular as she trotted on a loose rein before halting.

Aunt Sophie turned and watched them all. 'I'm going to put up a more difficult fence for you all to ride over once, but first, congrats to Pop for winning our little competition.'

Jessica's smile turned to a frown and it made Poppy feel uncomfortable.

'Thanks,' Poppy said, doing a little clap for herself, even though she was self-conscious about Jessica watching.

'I easily beat Poppy,' Jessica said. 'Hands down.'

Aunt Sophie's smile stayed fixed on her face and all Poppy could do was stare between her aunt and Jessica.

'You did a great round, Jessica, but Poppy didn't take a rail.'

'But I barely knocked it!' Jessica insisted. 'And my time was better.'

'I'm sorry, Jessica, but the rail fell down,' Aunt

Sophie said confidently. 'We're training for real competitions, girls, so I'm applying the same rules as any judge would.'

'That's not fair,' Jessica said with a pout. 'If your jump stands were better, that rail would have only rocked and not fallen.'

Poppy and Katie stayed silent, but Milly suddenly spoke up.

'The Ds have great jumps, and you don't see me moaning about coming last.'

'You're probably used to it,' Jessica said with a sneer.

'Excuse me?' Milly demanded.

Aunt Sophie held up her hand and stepped forward. 'Enough, girls. Now follow me into the ring while I change one of the jumps. This one will challenge all of you.'

Milly was still glaring at Jessica, and Jessica looked like she wanted to leap from her pony and have a full-on fist fight with Milly.

Poppy felt annoyed as the realisation hit her that, for the rest of holiday, they were going to have to put up with Jessica moaning and either being a sore loser or gloating about winning. Instead of being excited that she'd done so well and beaten both her friends, riders she admired, Poppy felt like she didn't deserve it, thanks to Jessica's outburst.

'I'm going to put the flower pots in front of the jumps, just like you might find in a real show-jumping competition, and also turn this upright into a spread,' Aunt Sophie told them.

Poppy tuned in to what her aunt was saying. She wanted to represent Australia one day and ride with the best riders in her country, and she knew that the only way that was going to happen was to listen to everything her aunt was teaching her, and absorb it all like a sponge sucking up every last drop of water, as her dad would have said.

'You need to keep your eyes trained over the jump like you always do,' Aunt Sophie continued. 'Head high, and ride your horse confidently towards it. I want your heels down and your back straight, and don't forget those nice releases when you're going over to make sure your horse has enough space to really stretch out.'

The second the jump was up and Aunt Sophie was out of the way, Jessica broke away from them and cantered toward it, her pony easily clearing it and hardly breaking stride as she landed on the other side of the fence.

'Excellent, Jessica, just wait for my say-so next time,' Aunt Sophie called out. 'Girls, canter in a circle and each of you break away from the group in turn and pop over.'

Poppy nudged Crystal back into a canter and glanced over her shoulder before splitting away from the others and heading toward the jump. She stared at the flowers then told herself off, but her hesitation confused her horse and Crystal put on her brakes, skidding to a halt instead of taking off. Poppy groaned. She was so busy worrying about Jessica and being annoyed that she'd let Crystal down.

'You're okay, Pops, just turn her away and try again,' Aunt Sophie instructed. 'She felt you hesitate and she stopped rather than taking off wrong and risking crashing. She's a clever pony.'

Poppy ran her hand down Crystal's neck to give her a quick pat. 'You're all right, girl. We can do it this time.'

Blocking everything else out, Poppy focused only on the feel of Crystal beneath her. She sat up straight and pointed her toward the big fence again.

It was easily one of the biggest she'd ever jumped, but she had nothing to be scared of. Her pony was clever and would look after her.

Poppy tuned in to the one-two-three-four beat of Crystal's canter, looked confidently ahead and kept her legs firm, heels down. Before she knew it they were mid-air, her position perfect, completely balanced, then landing on the other side and cantering off.

'We did it!' she whispered excitedly to Crystal, standing in her stirrups so she could pat her easily. 'I knew we could.'

Instead of forcing a smile at Jessica this time, Poppy ignored her completely, moving back into the circle the others were cantering in and falling in behind Katie as Milly broke away. She felt great. She'd just jumped a scarily high fence, and Crystal had made it seem easy.

'I know you're probably getting tired, but I want to finish with a bending pole race,' Aunt Sophie announced, pointing to where she had the poles set up. 'Just one race so we can keep the horses fresh, but the Pony Club kids will be pretty good at this game, and I want you all to be prepared.'

Poppy was tired, but she was also exhilarated still from the jumping.

'After this, I want you all to go on a nice walk around the farm with your horses. At least fifteen minutes for them to cool down and to stretch out their muscles since this is their first ride in almost a week. Just hold the reins on the buckle so they can really relax.'

Poppy rode over to the starting line with the others, and as soon as Crystal realised what they were doing she started to jig-jog. Poppy was sure it must have been the Arab in her that made her get so excited like this when all the other ponies were still just walking along like normal, especially after all the riding they'd already done.

As they neared the poles, Crystal started to snort, and she pawed the ground when Poppy asked her to halt at the start line.

'Okay, girls, remember not to miss a pole. Turn your pony fast at the end and go as quick as you can,' Aunt Sophie instructed. 'Ready, set...'

Crystal reared and, just like at the practice

gymkhana, Poppy had to spin her around and start the race backwards.

'… *Go!*'

Crystal spun back without Poppy having to do anything, half-rearing as she turned hard and raced toward the first pole. Poppy kept her reins firm, but Crystal knew what she was doing, nose out and moving side to side as she passed each pole, spinning hard at the end and doing the same on the way back. Poppy could see Jessica's bay pony from the corner of her eye, but she ignored her and just focused on Crystal, not wanting to miss a pole and go the wrong side of it. They passed the last one and raced toward the finish line. Crystal was grunting as she galloped so fast.

Yes! She'd done it! She'd actually won at the showjumping and the bending race. Maybe dreaming of getting a ribbon at the gymkhana wasn't so far-fetched after all.

'She shoved me!' Milly yelled. Poppy whipped her head around and saw anger written all over her friend's face.

'I did not,' Jessica replied, the scowl on her face taking Poppy by surprise, it was so nasty.

'Liar!' Milly accused.

'Enough,' Aunt Sophie said, hands on her hips. 'I will not have you fighting like that.'

The girls stayed silent. Poppy swapped glances with Katie.

'Congrats,' Katie mouthed.

'Thanks,' Poppy mouthed back silently.

'Jessica, I saw you shove Milly,' Aunt Sophie continued. 'Don't go pretending like it didn't happen. But Milly, some of the riders at the gymkhana might play dirty, and you have to be prepared for that.'

Milly was still glaring at Jessica, but it seemed the new girl didn't like being caught out. She looked beyond grumpy, Poppy thought.

'I didn't touch her,' Jessica continued, pouting.

'Poppy, you've done well today,' Aunt Sophie said, giving Poppy an exasperated look that made Poppy grin at her. 'You've all done well, shoving and arguing aside. Now go stretch those ponies out.'

But Jessica wasn't letting it go.

'I'm not going with them, and I want private lessons,' Jessica demanded. 'If I'm going to train in a group, I expect better riders to train against.'

Poppy burst out laughing but quickly clamped

her hand over her mouth. She looked at her friends. Katie was wide-eyed in disbelief, and Milly looked furious.

'No way,' Poppy muttered. Jessica was just a bad loser. She'd beaten her fair and square.

'Jessica, you're all very well matched. Any of you could have won today, it was a very fair contest.'

Jessica didn't say another word. Instead, she turned her horse and trotted off in a huff, slapping her on the rump as if everything was her fault.

'She's crazy,' Milly muttered. 'Absolutely cuckoo.' She twirled her finger in a circle round and round her ear, cuckooing as she did so. At the same time, some cockatoos screeched, and Poppy was sure the birds were calling back to Milly with her silly squawking noise.

'Have a nice ride, girls,' Aunt Sophie said, throwing them a smile before walking off. 'I need to go have a chat with our newest rider.'

Poppy had her feet out of the stirrups as she rode, and she was rolling her ankles in circles. Her legs were aching from being back in the saddle again, and she always liked to stretch out after jumping.

'How about we just don't talk about her?' Katie suggested.

'We've hardly talked about anything, anyway,' Milly said. 'It's like, I'm so shocked I can't even think of anything to say.'

'Well that's a first.' Poppy grinned, and suddenly everything felt back to normal again as the others visibly relaxed and smiled.

'Hey, look,' Katie whispered.

They turned and looked to where Katie was pointing. A kangaroo was watching them from the nearby paddock, and a big joey was leaning out of her pouch. The girls didn't ride too close to it, but they all halted, watching. The mother stared back at them, her nose twitching before she hopped a bit further away and continued to nibble.

Poppy never tired of seeing all the wild animals around the farm, especially the kangaroos. It always made her feel so special that she got to see them like this, wild and free.

'She shoved me hard,' Milly told them, her voice quiet and so unMillylike. 'I guess I just wasn't expecting it.'

'I thought we weren't talking about her,' Poppy said grimly.

'Yeah, I know, I just…'

Poppy didn't need Milly to finish her sentence; she knew what she meant and how she felt. They all sat on their halted horses, watching the kangaroo a while longer until she slowly moved further away, staying in the shade of the trees and keeping far enough from them to feel safe.

'Don't say you want to go home,' Poppy said quietly.

'Go home?' Milly squawked. 'I don't care what she does to me, there's no way I'm going home.'

Poppy breathed out a sigh of relief. 'Good. I don't want to be here without you two.'

'You know, we're definitely as good as her,' Katie said. 'I don't want to sound stuck up, but we are. She's got a gorgeous pony, but we've got awesome horses, too. They might not be as flashy, but they're ours and they're great, and we're great.'

Poppy watched as Milly nodded her head vigorously. 'Poppy beat her fair and square today.'

'Beginner's luck,' Poppy mumbled, embarrassed and happy at the same time.

'No, Pops, you were great today. We all were. I just need to speed up and Milly needs to take things a little slower. We can't let Jessica get in our heads and make out like she's better at everything when she's not.'

'So what do we do?' Poppy asked, not used to dealing with mean girls. At school, she and Sarah stuck together like glue, and most of the other girls were nice enough. So dealing with Jessica felt like figuring out how to deal with an alien.

'We just do what we've always done,' Katie said. 'We have fun and train hard.'

Milly grinned at them both. 'Or we figure out how to knock her off her high horse.'

Poppy and Katie groaned at the same time. Poppy hoped she didn't actually want to knock her off her pony. With Milly, you could never be sure.

'Not another one of your harebrained ideas, Mills. No way,' Poppy cautioned.

'Hey, who you calling harebrained?' she asked, giving a near-perfect impression of Jessica's evil pout.

'You,' Poppy said.

'I second it,' Katie announced, shaking her head.

'I'm not saying I've got anything planned,' Milly said, turning Joe around and starting to walk. '*Yet!*' she added mischievously.

Poppy pressed her legs to Crystal's side and fell into step alongside Katie, the pair of them riding so close their knees bumped.

'She's going to get us into trouble again, isn't she?' Poppy whispered.

'*Definitely*,' Katie whispered back. 'She's up to something.'

'I can hear you,' Milly called out, waving her hands above her head, reins loose around Joe's neck.

'Yeah, we know,' Poppy quipped. 'But no matter what we say, nothing's going to stop you, is it?'

'Nope,' Milly said with a giggle.

So they rode back to the stables, reins loose, stirrups hanging free, with Poppy worrying about what on earth her crazy friend was going to do. Aunt Sophie wouldn't let them off so easy this time if they did something stupid again. That was the only thing she was certain about right now.

CHAPTER FIVE

Trouble

'Yes, I understand,' Poppy heard Sophie say as her aunt held the phone to her ear and walked from the room into the other living room. 'There was an incident today, but…' She shut the door behind her and Poppy couldn't hear another word.

Milly sprung up beside her, and Poppy wriggled closer to Katie.

'You reckon that was Jessica's mum?' Milly asked.

Poppy nodded. 'Had to be.'

'Are we in trouble?' Katie asked. 'You never know what she's told her mum.'

Poppy stood up, wincing as her muscles tightened in her legs. She was sore from being back in the saddle, the inside of her thighs aching. They were sitting around in the living room chatting, the TV blaring on some boring show that her uncle had been watching before he'd gone to put the kettle on.

'Want to go down and say goodnight to the horses?' Poppy asked.

The others were on their feet and heading for the door as quickly as she was.

'We're just heading down to the horses for a bit,' Poppy called out to Uncle Mark, who looked deep in thought while dunking a tea bag in his oversized 'best uncle' mug.

'There's a bag of peppermints in that drawer there,' he said, pointing to one of the kitchen drawers. 'Take a few for the ponies as a treat, they'll love them.'

'Shouldn't you be telling us off for giving them sugary treats?' Katie asked. 'You know, since you're a vet?'

His laugh was loud. 'Yeah, probably. Just don't tell anyone it was my idea, okay?'

Poppy found the mints and took a handful, dropping a few first into Milly's outstretched hand, then Katie's. She popped one in her mouth as they headed out the door, reaching for her boots that she'd kicked off outside. She gave them a quick shake to check for spiders then wiggled her feet in.

'Wait up!'

Mark's call made them all stop, and her uncle came jogging down the steps after them, his hand fisted. She guessed he had some mints, too.

'I haven't seen much of Shadow lately. Poor old boy will think I don't love him anymore.'

Shadow was her uncle's horse, a beautiful big pinto that he'd had for years. He was huge, with long white hair called feathers that grew down over part of his hooves because he was half shire.

Milly was asking Mark question after question about being a vet, and Mark was giving her all the gruesome details.

'Can we come along with you one day when you're doing something fun?' Milly asked.

Katie gasped, excited. 'I want to be a vet when I grow up. Please, Mr D, that would be so amazing.'

Poppy didn't say anything. She had always tagged along with her uncle on call-outs when she stayed in the past, only this time she'd been so busy with her friends that she hadn't asked him. He'd always told her she had to be quiet and not get in the way when she went, so she was guessing that three of them might be too much for him to take out on rounds.

'What is it that you think will be fun?' he asked with an arched eyebrow, pulling a comical face as the cockatoos commenced their screeching rounds, flocking from one tree to another and covering the sky with their beating wings. It was the time of night Poppy liked best, when the sun started to fade and cast a golden light over everything it touched.

'Maybe some sort of exciting animal rescue,' Milly continued, raising her voice to be heard above the cockatoos. 'You know, where you get called in and save the day.'

Uncle Mark chuckled. 'I hate to break it to you girls, but you're more likely to find me with my arm stuck up a cow's bottom or stitching up horses' legs after they have a run-in with a wire fence.'

'Ewww,' Milly and Katie groaned at the same time.

Poppy just smiled. She'd seen Uncle Mark with his arm stuck up to his shoulder inside big animals more times than she could count, and it wasn't pretty to watch. But the way he helped first-time cow- and horse-mums give birth was pretty special.

'Do you at least wear a glove?' Milly asked, clearly grossed out.

He slung his arm around her. 'Yes, Mils, I wear a very long glove. And yes, you can come with me one day. I'll even give you your own glove to wear.'

Poppy laughed as Milly visibly shuddered. 'I think I'll pass,' Milly said.

Poppy swung the door to the stables open and flicked on the light as soon as they entered. The smell of manure and hay and horse hit her nostrils the second she entered, making her smile. And when some of the horses nickered out, it made her smile even wider.

'It wasn't so long ago that you girls were sleeping down here, protecting your ponies,' Uncle Mark said as he followed her in, chuckling. 'Hopefully you'll be able to stay in your own beds this time round.'

Poppy smiled at the memory. It felt like forever ago and it was only a couple of weeks!

'Are you still angry with us about sneaking off to Old Smithy's place?' Katie asked.

'Angry? No way. I still wish you'd told us, but I'm proud of you girls for being so gutsy and determined. There's not enough people in this world sticking up for animals.'

Poppy let herself into Crystal's stall, but the mare was pacing around the loosebox and pawing at the sawdust, stopping only when she realised Poppy had something for her. Poppy frowned. Crystal was usually so calm. Something was up.

'Hey, it's okay,' Poppy soothed. 'What's got you all upset?'

Crystal kept her head down and snuffled the peppermints off Poppy's palm while she stroked her pony's neck. Poppy glanced around the stable and noticed that Crystal's hay bag was completely empty. She wiped her damp hands on her jods and stared at the bag, checking the ground to make sure all the hay hadn't somehow fallen out, but there was no feed for her poor horse anywhere.

She was starting to wonder if she was going crazy when Katie poked her nose over the door.

'You wouldn't believe it, but Cody's eaten all of his hay.'

Poppy pointed toward Crystal's. 'Crystal, too.

I know I filled it up with at least three biscuits. She should have had enough to last her until the early hours of the morning.'

'There's something weird going on,' Katie said.

'Hey, you guys…' Milly started calling out.

'Girls, what have I told you about making sure your horses have enough hay to last the night?' Mark asked, his tone angry as he interrupted Milly. Poppy wasn't used to hearing him sound angry. *Ever.* 'If they're in overnight, they need ample hay. Their stomachs aren't designed to go for long periods without feed. You should know this.'

Milly appeared from behind Uncle Mark. Her shoulders were bunched up and she looked worried.

'You too, Poppy?' Mark shook his head. 'You've been doing this long enough to know better.'

Uncle Mark was standing at the door to Crystal's stable, and Poppy came closer to him. 'I promise I filled her hay bag up. We all did,' Poppy said defensively. 'I couldn't even eat my own dinner if I thought Crystal was down here hungry.'

His gaze softened, like he believed her. 'It's not like any of you not to care for your horses properly,' he said, confusion etching a crease into his forehead.

Poppy let herself out of Crystal's stable, careful to clasp the door behind her. 'This is going to sound crazy, but something weird is going on. We all fed our horses, hand on my heart.'

'I would never leave Joe hungry,' Milly agreed, and Katie had her arms wrapped around herself as she nodded, too.

Uncle Mark looked like he didn't know what to say, as if he didn't know whether he believed them or not. 'Refill their hay bags now, and look in on all the others to make sure they're full. We'll talk about this later.'

Poppy stood still and so did the others, watching as Uncle Mark went back to his horse, gave him a pat and a final mint, then left the stables. Poppy knew he'd be going back to the house to tell her aunt and see what she thought, and she only hoped that Aunt Sophie knew she'd never leave Crystal without food.

'Jessica's horse has plenty of feed,' Katie called out.

Milly leaned over Joe's stable door, her nose all wrinkled up like she'd smelt something bad. '*She* did it.'

Katie groaned from further down the aisle, at Cody's stall. 'Don't go jumping to conclusions.'

'I know you're thinking the same thing as me, you just don't want to say it,' Milly shot straight back.

'I think Milly's right,' Poppy said quietly, leaning her back against Joe's stall. 'How else could it have happened?'

'So you both think that she came in here and took all the hay out of the bags, just to get back at us for winning today?' Katie asked.

Poppy nodded glumly.

'Yep,' Milly said. 'There's no other explanation.'

Poppy smiled as Joe popped his head over the stable door. The doors were low enough that even the ponies could comfortably hang their heads over, and she tickled Joe on the chin. His lips moved and he snuffled her hair.

'Would she be that mean?' Katie asked.

Milly scoffed. 'You've seen her smack her horse for doing nothing wrong. Of course she'd be that mean. So what are we going to do about it? We can't just let her get away with it.'

'We can't go doing anything crazy without

thinking it through first,' Poppy cautioned. 'But if she did do this, that's more than mean – it's plain cruel. No matter how bad things get, we have to be sure before we accuse her of anything. Aunt Sophie's pretty understanding, but I don't think we'll get away with just a telling off again if we do something stupid.'

'What if we catch her red-handed?' Milly asked, eyes wide.

'How?' Poppy asked.

'I'm not sure. But we have to do something.'

They all trudged off to the big stable that was used to store the hay, and came back with armfuls, filling their ponies' bags and all making sure the doors were secure. Poppy checked Crystal's water, too, making sure everything was as it should be in the loosebox before giving her pony a final pat goodnight.

'See you in the morning,' Poppy said, dropping a kiss to the soft, darker grey part of Crystal's muzzle. 'Love you.'

She joined the other two and they headed back toward the house. It was almost completely dark now, and Katie squealed when a bat made a loud noise. Poppy grabbed her hand and pointed up at a nearby tree where five flying foxes were hanging and jostling for space. All of a sudden, one burst away from the group, its distinct bat outline just visible against the dark skyline.

'There must be something nice around here for them to eat,' Poppy told her.

'Like me?' Katie asked with a quiver in her voice.

'They're harmless,' Poppy assured her. 'They eat berries and things, and they're pretty cute when you look at them up close. You see them, Milly?'

Milly planted her hands on her hips. 'I don't care about bats right now. Someone tried to starve my horse to death, and I want to catch her out.'

CHAPTER SIX

Riding with Jessica

Poppy was lying in bed, trying to fall asleep. She'd wriggled into every possible position trying to get comfortable, and pulled the covers up higher, but nothing was working. A slither of light slipped into the room from the doorway, and she peeked out from beneath her doona.

She saw Aunt Sophie bend over Milly first and then Katie, pulling a blanket that had slipped down higher over Katie. Then she turned and headed toward Poppy.

'Pops?' Aunt Sophie whispered. 'What are you doing awake?'

Poppy realised she'd been holding her breath, so

she quickly blew it out.

'I can't sleep,' she said.

Aunt Sophie sat on the bed, her weight making Poppy roll toward her a little.

'You're upset over finding the horses with no feed, aren't you? Mark told me what happened.'

Tears sprung into Poppy's eyes, and she bit down hard on her lip, trying to stop them from spilling. 'I didn't do it,' she whispered back. 'I would never ever leave Crystal or any of the horses to go hungry.'

Aunt Sophie leaned down and wrapped her arms around her. She smelt nice, like horses and perfume, and her long hair was loose and fell against Poppy's face. Her aunt had given her so many cuddles at home when she'd been looking after her while her mum was away, and there was something so comforting about Sophie. Or maybe it was just because she'd craved her mum's snuggles for months, and so snuggles from Sophie were the next best thing. Poppy buried her face in Sophie's hair, and hoped her brother was getting the cuddles she knew he sometimes needed before bed.

'Sometimes we can get busy with other things

and forget our most important tasks. It's okay to make a mistake, Poppy,' Sophie said.

Poppy pulled away from her aunt. 'But I didn't forget,' she insisted, staring into her aunt's eyes, needing her to know that it wasn't her fault. 'I know how to look after horses. You've taught me, and I wouldn't do that. I wouldn't just forget.'

'I'm not angry with you, Pops. It's okay.' Aunt Sophie whispered as she dropped a kiss to her forehead. 'See you in the morning. Just try to get a good night's sleep.'

Poppy pulled the covers back up, this time making sure they went right over her face. She wouldn't cry. Crying was for super-sad things like thinking about her dad or dealing with her mum when she was so bad Poppy couldn't even get her out of bed. Her dad would have been brave if something like this had happened to him, being blamed for something he hadn't done, and she needed to be, too. Aunt Sophie wasn't angry with her, but that still didn't make it okay when she hadn't made a mistake in the first place. She was so frustrated with the whole thing that she just wanted to scream!

She wiped at her eyes and took a deep breath.

Milly was right. If Jessica had done this, they needed to prove it. No way was Poppy going to let her get away with it.

The next morning, Poppy never said a word to the others about talking to Aunt Sophie, because then she'd have to tell them that she was certain Sophie didn't believe them. They'd already mucked out the stables, double-checked all the horses' feed, and Poppy was now sitting on an overturned bucket outside Crystal's stable, checking everything was in order with all her gear. She wasn't going to let anyone mess with her horse *or* her things.

'Uh-oh,' Milly said with a groan. She was sitting nearby doing the same thing as Poppy. 'I think we're in trouble.'

Poppy looked up and saw Jessica striding down the middle of the stable building with her mum. They were heading straight for them. Her mother had perfect hair, perfect make-up, perfect clothes, but in a don't-even-think-about-touching-me kind of way; the complete opposite of Aunt Sophie. Sophie was always immaculate, but her hair was soft and touchable, her mouth always smiling, and she never seemed to care about getting her hands dirty.

'Are these the girls?' Jessica's mum demanded when they stopped next to Poppy and Milly.

Poppy gulped as Katie stepped out of Cody's stable. They were definitely in some sort of trouble.

'Yes,' Jessica said, one hand on her hip.

Poppy's fingers tensed around the brush she was holding. She exchanged quick glances with Milly and Katie, who both looked worried.

'Jessica has been telling me that you girls haven't been very welcoming,' her mother began. 'I understand that it can be hard having someone new arrive, but I'd appreciate you trying to include my daughter. The way you've been treating her is completely unacceptable.'

Poppy had to clamp her mouth shut to stop her jaw from falling open. *Them* not nice to *her?*

Aunt Sophie walked out of the tack room just as Milly took a few steps forward.

'What's going on here?' Aunt Sophie said. 'Mrs Perkins, is there a problem that we didn't discuss over the phone last night?'

'I was just telling these girls that I don't appreciate

the way they've been excluding poor Jessica.'

Milly laughed, but Poppy just stared at Jessica's mum. How could they be the ones accused of being mean? Her face felt burning hot, she was so mad.

'I think it's best to discuss this in private, Mrs Perkins. As I said, the girls have been most welcoming to Jessica. In fact, I was going to suggest they all go on a trail ride this morning.'

'But she stole our horses' hay and left them with nothing last night!' Poppy suddenly blurted, not able to stop herself. 'We know it was her.'

'Poppy, that's enough!' Aunt Sophie scolded.

'She did,' Milly said, sticking up for her.

'Go and saddle up your horses, girls. I don't want to hear any more wild accusations,' Sophie told them in her no-nonsense voice.

'This is exactly what I'm talking about, Sophie. I can't see why you even have these girls here, the way they carry on.'

Poppy stormed off to get her gear, not looking at Jessica but quickly linking her arm through Katie's as she saw tears in her friend's eyes. Poppy knew exactly how her friend felt. She was so frustrated at not being able to do anything about Jessica, and being blamed for something that wasn't her fault.

'Don't,' Poppy whispered as they followed Milly into the tack room. 'Don't let her get to you.'

'But how can she say that we're the…'

'No tears,' Poppy ordered, interrupting her and swinging the tack room door shut behind them. 'We're going to catch her out. Milly was right – we have to do something, but we have to be clever about it, and that means pretending everything's fine until we figure out a way to catch her in the act.'

The door creaked open. Poppy slung her bridle over her shoulder and reached for her saddle, carrying it over both arms. When she walked out, she saw Jessica standing there with a smug smile on her face.

Poppy didn't say a word. She kept walking, put her saddle over her stable door and let herself in, throwing her arms around Crystal and hugging her tight. But even the sweet smell of her horse and the gentle muzzle against her side wasn't enough to make her forget about Jessica.

The trail stretched out ahead of them, and Poppy looked back at the others. She was leading them single file through the tighter part of the track, but it was about to become wider and it was her favourite spot to canter. The ground was soft beneath them, covered in pine needles and a heavy smattering of fallen blue gum leaves, so they didn't have to worry about it being too hard for their horses' hooves.

'Ready?' Poppy called out.

'Yep, let's canter!' Milly called back, always eager to go faster.

Poppy touched her heels to Crystal's sides and pushed her into a trot, then a canter, loving the bouncy gait of her horse beneath her. The track was easily wide enough for two of them to ride side by side, and Milly pulled up beside her. As usual, Joe was racing to get his nose in front of Crystal's, desperate to be in front. Poppy giggled and gave Crystal a bit more rein to speed up, knowing she loved the race, too.

The trees weren't as dense now, but there were still blue gums lining each side of the track, and Poppy felt Crystal pull for her head, anticipating the jump ahead. The trail narrowed again, and there was the fallen tree blocking the path. They always jumped it, the trunk almost perfectly white from where the bark had all peeled away.

'Jump ahead!' she called out, warning Katie and Jessica behind them. Jessica hadn't been out with them before, and although Poppy didn't like her, she didn't want her to be unprepared and fall.

They rounded the corner and kept cantering, and Poppy reined back to let Milly take the lead. But Crystal wasn't keen on slowing, and they ended up flying over the jump as a perfect pair.

'Awesome!' Milly squealed.

Poppy couldn't stop grinning. 'We could enter those competitions where you have to jump the entire course as a double act,' she called out.

They slowed to a trot when the track narrowed, and Poppy took the lead again. It was hot out today, but it was always nice under the shady canopy of the trees, their highest branches crisscrossing above and making a haphazard kind of umbrella above them.

Poppy let herself look around. She peered into the highest branches, remembering how she used to see so many koalas when she first started riding with her aunt. They were hard to spot though now, with so few around. She hoped they were just hiding and hadn't ended up by the road where they could be hit by a car.

Crystal suddenly slammed on her brakes, letting out a loud snort as dust came flying up from her back hooves. Poppy grabbed hold of a fistful of white mane, saving herself from falling just in time.

'Whoa, girl,' she soothed, frantically trying to thrust her foot back through the stirrup that she'd lost as she jerked to the side.

'No!' she cried as Crystal suddenly reared up, flinging out her front hooves and pawing at the air. Poppy could only hold on for so long, her balance slipping as Crystal reared up even higher.

Poppy felt herself be thrown off to the side, and she fell hard, landing on her hip. Her left arm flung out and hit something hard.

'Ow!' she cried, but rolled to the side of the trail fast, throwing both hands over her head as she ducked to get out of Crystal's way. She peeked through her arms when she heard the sound of hooves, worried about being trampled by the others, but she couldn't see them so figured she must be hearing things.

Her eyes bulged when something moved on the ground next to her. It was a massive black snake, and it slithered straight past Poppy, disappearing into the bush. No wonder poor Crystal had spooked! She kept her eyes on the snake as hooves thundered down the track behind her.

'Pops! You okay?' Milly called, first to leap off her horse and reach her.

'Poppy!' Katie was calling. 'Poppy!'

'Get Crystal,' she whispered. She was winded, and it was hard for her to even catch her breath.

Katie rode further down the track after Crystal while Milly extended a hand out to Poppy. 'Come on, up you get before that snake comes back.'

'I didn't know what she was spooking at,' Poppy admitted, 'until it came straight past me just then.'

Milly visibly shuddered. 'It wasn't her fault. I think it went straight under her hooves.'

Poppy swallowed, still in shock. She'd never fallen off Crystal before, and her arm was throbbing. But Milly was right, it wasn't Crystal's fault. Any horse would have freaked out with a snake slithering around beneath them.

'Are you okay?' Milly asked, looking worried. 'How bad are you hurt?'

'I've got Crystal,' Katie called out. 'But Jessica's gone.'

Poppy forgot all about her arm for a second. She looked around and saw that it was just the three of them. 'What do you mean, she's gone?'

'She just rode off like nothing had happened. That's why Crystal kept going, I think she was just wanting to catch up with Jessica's horse. She must have cantered past you when you fell.'

Poppy winced when she stretched out her arm, but she thought that it was already starting to feel a little better than before. She lifted up her top and pushed down the waistband of her jods to look at her hip. It was red, and there was the start of an ugly purple bruise.

'I can't believe she'd just ride off like that,' Poppy muttered, dropping her T-shirt back down. 'That's low, even for her.'

'Need a leg up?' Milly asked.

Poppy shook her head, checking Crystal over to make sure she was okay. She took the reins from Katie, who was still mounted on Cody and stroking Crystal's neck.

'It's okay. I know you didn't mean it,' Poppy told her horse. Even the most confident horse in the world could be startled by something, which was why Aunt Sophie insisted they wear helmets whenever they were on horseback.

She pushed her left foot into the stirrup and bounced on her right before swinging up, crying out when the movement sent a jolt up her hip. She moved carefully to avoid any more pain. She'd be fine, but she knew her bruises would be nasty.

'We need to go and find Jessica,' Poppy said.

'She can find her own way back. I'm not going looking for her,' Milly declared.

'Yeah, and then we'll end up with the blame and she'll look like Miss Perfect,' Katie said.

Poppy winced again as she shifted her weight and tried to get comfortable. 'Come on. I'm going to text Aunt Sophie now and tell her that Jessica rode off on her own, just to make sure she doesn't go riding back saying that we left her. Then we can go looking for her.'

Milly shrugged and Katie nodded, so Poppy quickly messaged her aunt, clipped the phone back in the waistband of her jods and nudged Crystal with her legs. They set off at a walk, then moved into a trot. Poppy gritted her teeth, refusing to give in to the pain in her side. She decided she wasn't going to tell Sophie how bad it hurt because then she might not let her ride for a few days, and there was no way she was missing out on even one ride.

'I bet she's up here,' Milly called, in the lead and taking the wider track to the right. The only other option was a narrow path with low-hanging, scratchy branches. 'She would have taken the easy one.'

Milly suddenly held up her hand and slowed down. 'Up ahead,' she called over her shoulder.

Poppy peered past Milly and Joe, and saw Jessica's horse tethered loosely to a branch by her reins. But where was Jessica?

'Where is she?' Katie asked.

'Jessica,' Poppy yelled out. 'Jessica!'

Jessica suddenly appeared from up ahead, pushing branches out of her way. Maybe they'd underestimated her curiosity, because she had obviously been exploring and didn't care about getting scratched. 'I was just taking a look around. Thought I'd find another snake for Poppy.'

Poppy's face burned hot and she bet her cheeks were bright red, but she bit down on her lip and didn't say anything back.

'I thought you hated trail riding,' Milly quipped.

'And I'd love to see your horse stay calm with a snake slithering around her hooves.'

Jessica scowled. 'So did you come to rescue me or something? Because I don't need your help.'

'Come on, let's just get back before Mrs D sends out the rescue team,' Katie muttered, turning Cody around and bumping knees with Poppy.

Poppy took a big breath and mustered all her courage, still facing Jessica. She wasn't used to having confrontations – she usually just got on with things – but she wasn't letting Jessica get away with what she'd just done. 'We have a few rules here at Starlight,' she said. 'First is you always tell someone where you're going riding, and the second is that if you're riding with a buddy, you never leave them if they fall.'

Jessica shrugged. 'My bad. Sorry.'

Poppy pushed her shoulders back and spun Crystal around, riding off with the others and leaving Jessica trying to scramble up while her horse anxiously stamped her feet. Poppy bet the mare hated not being able to follow the other horses home, and she had to shut her eyes and say a silent sorry when she heard her get a smack with the whip.

But if Jessica didn't want to be part of their team, that was her problem. Poppy was just sorry it made it poor Cleopatra's problem, too.

'Girls! Thank goodness you're back.' Aunt Sophie ran out to them, dressed in her usual outfit of cream jods and a pink shirt, her long hair woven into a fish plait and hanging loosely over her shoulder. 'I was just saddling one of the horses up to come find you.'

'We're fine,' Poppy told her, halting Crystal and dismounting. 'Sorry we took so long.'

'Jessica, did you ride off on your own?' Aunt Sophie asked.

'Yes.' Jessica's voice was so sweet it made Poppy want to be sick. 'I didn't know the rules. Sorry.'

'I fell off,' Poppy said, changing her mind about not telling Sophie. There was no way she was going to let Jessica speak first and spin some stupid story to make what she'd done sound okay. Poppy held up her T-shirt to show the bruise that had spread across her hip and her side. Her aunt needed to see that what had happened was serious so that she knew how awful Jessica had been to ride off. Showing her the bruise would at least shock her into listening! 'There was a snake on the track and I was leading, but when the other girls stopped, Jessica just rode off on her own. Once I got back on we had to go find her. That's when I messaged you.'

'I have to say, I'm disappointed that you wouldn't stop for your fellow rider and make sure she was okay, Jessica. But I'm glad you're okay, Pops. How bad does it hurt?'

Poppy shrugged. It hurt like crazy but she wasn't saying so in case Sophie stopped her from riding! 'It did hurt, but it's fine now.'

Poppy looked over and saw that her friends had dismounted, too, so she led Crystal back into the stables to take her horse's gear off.

'Hose them all down since it's such a hot day, and let them out into one of the paddocks,' Aunt Sophie called after them. 'Pops, could you put Jupiter in with the ponies for a bit when you get a chance?'

'Yep, sure thing,' Poppy called back before disappearing into the cool of the stables. The sun was super hot today. She took her helmet off and felt her hair, all damp with sweat due to wearing the hat.

'You did great out there, Poppy,' Katie told her, high-fiving her as she walked past.

'Thanks.' She couldn't help grinning, even though Jessica was following right behind her.

'But you're so lying about that fall not hurting, aren't you?' Milly asked, raising one eyebrow and making her laugh.

'It hurts so bad I could hardly walk without limping out there,' she admitted.

Milly made a sad face and blew her a kiss, and Poppy pretended to catch it and press it against her side. Poppy laughed with her friends, and ignored Jessica who she was sure she just saw roll her eyes at them.

Katie had been right all along – they just had to have fun and pretend like Jessica wasn't even there, and one day, they'd be able to prove to Aunt Sophie just how mean Jessica really was.

CHAPTER SEVEN

Everything Goes Wrong

The sun was so hot that it was making sweat bead across Poppy's forehead. She dropped her shovel and walked over to the water trough, bending down and scooping up water to splash on her face. It was cold and instantly made her feel better.

'That's gross,' Katie called out.

Poppy shrugged. 'I kept my mouth shut!' She didn't care, it was only the horses that drank out of it, and she'd share anything with Crystal. Besides, they'd only cleaned it out the day before, so it was crystal clear.

'My arms are killing me,' Milly moaned, throwing her shovel down and lying on the grass.

They'd mucked out three paddocks so far, and after riding all morning and cleaning the stables out, they were all exhausted. Poppy went over and sat down next to Milly, arms resting on her knees.

'Poppy!' An ear-splitting scream made her scramble to her feet.

'Was that Aunt Sophie?' she asked, looking at the others. Her mouth went dry again, panic surged through her body. Something was wrong. Aunt Sophie *never* screamed like that!

'GIRLS!'

Poppy burst into a run, arms pumping at her sides as she ran across the paddock and back toward the stables from where she thought she'd heard Sophie's voice. Then a flash of something in one of the paddocks caught her eye, and she screeched to a stop, boots digging into the dirt as she turned.

It was Joe!

'Milly, hurry!' Poppy yelled over her shoulder as she ran as fast as she could toward where her aunt was on the other side of their ponies' paddock.

Joe was careering around the paddock with his cover right over his head. It was a light summer sheet, they were all wearing them to keep the flies and the sun off them, but his was loose and flapping around the faster he raced. Crystal was pacing down one side of the paddock and Cody was watching, agitated. But Jupiter looked like he was about to join in with Joe, getting in a panic and starting to canter after him.

'No!' screamed Milly, overtaking Poppy, jumping the gate and landing in the paddock with the horses.

Aunt Sophie called out from the other side, frantically trying to stop Jupiter from the middle of the paddock. He finally stopped, snorting and pawing at the ground, and her aunt managed to grab him at the same time as Joe let out a frantic whinny as he ran straight into the fence, hitting it at full speed and flipping straight over it. Poppy's heart leapt as she watched the horror unfold, not knowing what to do.

'Joe!' Milly's scream was ear-splitting. 'Noooo!'

Milly was running so fast, and Poppy just stood there, trying to think how she could help. Then she saw Sophie trying to keep hold of Jupiter, so Poppy quickly jumped the fence to take him. Luckily she'd left all their halters on so he was easy to hold on to, and she gripped the leather tight. Her heart was pounding so loud, her breath ragged, but she forced herself to calm down so at least Jupiter wouldn't freak out more. She knew how much energy a horse took from its handler, so she needed to try to relax.

'Get the other two,' Poppy called to Katie. She stroked Jupiter's nose, keeping an eye on Crystal, who was looking extremely distressed. She watched Aunt Sophie catch up with Milly and attempt to help Joe. Part of the fence was mangled and half down from where Joe had damaged it. Poppy turned to Katie and acted instinctively. They needed to get all the horses out, and to somewhere safe and secure.

Poppy looked back to Joe. Aunt Sophie gently pulled his leg from the fence and he kicked out from where he was lying. Poppy gasped as she watched. Poor Joe's body was quivering as Milly gently coaxed him to his feet, and Poppy could see from where she was standing how hard he was blowing, too.

Aunt Sophie stepped forward and carefully unbuckled the front of Joe's cover, and pulled it to the ground. As Poppy watched her aunt check over Joe, all she could think was thank goodness they had the special plastic-coated horse fencing and not wire, otherwise his leg would have been shredded.

'Get those horses into the next paddock and

come over here immediately,' Aunt Sophie called out, her voice deep with anger.

Poppy led Jupiter over to the gate, and followed Katie with Crystal and Cody into the next paddock. Once all the horses were calm, the two girls walked in silence back to where Sophie and Milly were helping Joe. Poppy had a bad, terrible, horrible feeling that somehow they were about to get in a power-load of trouble, even though they'd done absolutely nothing wrong.

'Do you have any idea how lucky we are that Joe isn't being put down right now?' Aunt Sophie fumed.

Uncle Mark turned and frowned, shaking his head. 'He's fine, Sophie. We all need to calm down.'

Poppy felt awful for Joe and Milly. Her friend was sobbing, tears streaming down her cheeks as she held Joe's lead rope. From where Poppy was standing, she could see that his knee was swollen and he had a cut on his leg from when he'd been scrambling to stand up. But otherwise, Poppy was relieved to see that he was remarkably okay.

Sophie looked up and Poppy couldn't hold her

gaze. Sophie was so angry with them, but they hadn't done anything wrong! Poppy stared down at her boots and reached out to find Katie's hand. The two girls were standing so close that their shoulders were touching. Poppy found Katie's fingers and squeezed her hand as she heard Katie start to cry, too.

Poppy was holding it together, but only because she was so angry. She figured she'd shed enough tears to last her a lifetime when her dad had died.

'He needs a few days of rest. We'll keep icing that knee, and watch it closely, but otherwise he's fine,' Uncle Mark said, running a hand down Joe's shoulder and patting him. 'This is a very good lesson in why it's so important to secure the leg straps first before ever doing the front of the cover up.'

'But Milly knows that,' Poppy said, sticking up for her friend. 'None of us would ever make a mistake that stupid.' She couldn't just stand there and not say anything.

'Then how do you explain the fact that the back straps were still clipped to the rug?' Aunt Sophie asked, arms crossed angrily over her chest. 'If they'd just come undone, they would be hanging down, or broken from him catching them on something.'

They all stayed silent. Poppy knew who'd done this, and she couldn't believe that even someone mean like Jessica could be so cruel.

'I promise, Mrs D,' Milly said in a voice so low and quiet it didn't sound a bit like her. 'I know I secured the straps. I love Joe so much, and I'm so careful with him.'

Aunt Sophie turned to Mark. 'I don't know what to do. But, girls,' she said, looking back at them, 'unless you stop making silly mistakes and change your attitude toward Jessica, then none of you will be attending Pony Club or going to the gymkhana.'

Uncle Mark slung an arm around Aunt Sophie and walked her away a few steps. Poppy was numb all over, and she hated to think how Milly must feel right now. She was still holding Katie's hand so she dragged her over to Milly and they both threw their arms around her.

'You know I didn't do this, don't you?' Milly gasped, tears streaming again.

'I know,' Poppy said quickly. '*She* did this, it's the only explanation. She's got it in for you.'

'You know what this means,' Katie said, stroking Joe's neck and staring at Poppy. 'This is war.'

CHAPTER EIGHT

Brainstorming

Poppy hated seeing Milly so miserable. As punishment for what happened, and while Joe recovered, Milly had sat on Aunt Sophie's fold-out chair and watched them all through their riding lessons for the last five days, glumly looking on as Poppy, Katie and Jessica practised for the gymkhana show jumping. It had been even worse the day before, when they'd been out trail riding without her. Milly had waved to them, but Poppy could see how upset she was. They all could. And what was worse – Jessica seemed to be enjoying every second of Milly's misery.

The lesson was over, and Poppy slipped her feet from the stirrups and stretched out her legs, giving

Crystal a big pat as they rode out of the arena. They'd done okay today, but Jessica had blitzed them, doing two clear rounds and beating them all against the stopwatch. If she could just forget about her, she'd be fine, but every time Poppy looked at Milly, moping and looking so sad, she was reminded of everything that had happened since Jessica had arrived.

'How's Joe?' Poppy asked as she halted next to Milly and dismounted.

'Mr D's on his way over now to take a look at him,' Milly said, her eyes darting in the direction of the stables, where Joe was. 'The swelling in his leg has gone and he seems fine, but I won't know until he watches me trot him out and checks him.'

Poppy saw the evil stare Milly gave Jessica as the other girl rode straight past them.

Poppy nodded. 'I bet he'll be fine and you'll be riding with us again tomorrow.' She wasn't actually as confident as she sounded, but Milly seemed so anxious already that she wasn't going to tell her that.

'I stuffed up that round,' Katie said, joining them. 'I just need to stop being so careful and slow, and let Cody go faster.'

The girls went back to the stables to untack their horses. Milly came in to help Poppy, taking Crystal's saddle off and brushing her down. Poppy took Crystal's bridle off and used the softer brush on her face.

'I'm going to hose Cody down,' Katie called out from her loosebox.

Poppy raised a questioning eyebrow at Milly, hoping to include her friend in something at least a little bit fun, but Milly just shrugged back at her.

'Come on, you can squirt Crystal down while I hold her,' Poppy said.

They led the horses outside, and Milly grabbed the hose before Katie could, putting her finger over the end to make the water squirt harder, just like Poppy always did to get the sweat off Crystal's coat properly. Poppy was patting Crystal but then shut her eyes and tipped her head back to feel the sun on her face, leaning into her pony's soft neck.

A surge of cold water on her face made her eyes blink open in surprise. 'Aargh!' she squealed, jumping back and grappling to keep hold of the lead rope. She glared at the culprit holding the hosepipe. 'Milly!' She was innocently squirting Crystal's legs now, but she was grinning like crazy.

Poppy looked down at her T-shirt. It was her favourite pink one with a big horseshoe on the front, and now it was dripping wet at the front, same as her hair.

'Milly, just because...' Katie was cut off by a powerful spray of water from the hosepipe. She turned her back on Milly, squealing and trying to get away from the cold water.

The girls were now in fits of giggles, and Poppy quickly tied Crystal up and pounced on Milly, grabbing the hose from her and desperately trying to squirt her back.

'Sorry to break up the fun girls.'

Poppy let go of Milly and spun round at the sound of Uncle Mark's deep voice.

'We were just...'

'Having fun,' Uncle Mark finished her sentence for her, smiling. 'Wet me and I'll kill you, though.'

He indicated for Milly to go with him, and Poppy and Katie fell silent again. Poppy picked up the hose and finished hosing Crystal down, then passed it to Katie and used the scraper to take the excess water off Crystal's coat.

'Do you really think she'll be able to compete on Joe?' Katie asked in a quiet voice.

Poppy shrugged. 'I don't know. I hope so.'

They were both silent again, looking up when Milly led Joe out on to the concrete. Milly looked scared, and Poppy wished she could do something to make her feel better. Aunt Sophie appeared in the open entrance to the stables, watching intently.

'I want you to trot him out on the concrete in a straight line so I can do a proper lameness test,' Uncle Mark instructed. 'Then turn him around and trot straight back. I need you to do that a few times for me, so I can watch him.'

Poppy and Katie watched as Milly did as she was told, running back and forth alongside Joe. Mark finally told Milly that she could stop. Milly was panting, but Joe looked like he was just starting for the day with his ears pricked and tail swishing. Poppy bet he was bored silly from being locked up all day, every day in the stable, not doing anything.

Uncle Mark waved Aunt Sophie over and spoke to her. Poppy couldn't hear what they were saying, and from the look Milly gave her she didn't know what was being said either. Poppy crossed her fingers and leaned into Crystal.

'Milly, come here, please,' Aunt Sophie called.

Poppy couldn't tell what Sophie was thinking. She didn't even know if Sophie was still angry with them. She'd been so much quieter than usual since Joe's accident, and she'd hardly spoken to them except in training in the arena, but the smile on her face now made Poppy's heart start to race. It had to be good news, it just had to be!

'Come on, girls,' Aunt Sophie encouraged, waving Poppy and Katie over, probably knowing they were hanging off her every word, Poppy guessed. 'Tie them up there and join us.'

Poppy did a quick release knot and tied Crystal to the post before racing over to stand by Milly, who was biting down hard on her bottom lip like she was about to chew it off.

'Joe looks great,' Uncle Mark confirmed. 'I want you to take it easy on him, Milly. I'm going to check him every day, just in case, but he's not lame and his leg is fine. And there's no swelling that I can see.'

'Thank you, thank you, thank you!' Milly leapt forward and flung her arms around Mark's neck, almost knocking him over, she hit him so suddenly.

Uncle Mark laughed, and then Milly was flinging herself at Sophie.

'How about you give him a light ride later this afternoon with the girls,' Sophie said. 'Just a big walk around the farm or on a trail ride, and then you can join lessons again tomorrow. We only have a few days left to prepare for the gymkhana, and I don't want you to miss out.'

Milly spun around, squealing with excitement. Poppy couldn't hold back any longer – she threw her arms around Milly and Katie, hugging her friends hard in relief and excitement, and jumped up and down.

'I knew he'd be fine,' Poppy said, even though she'd secretly been terrified he wouldn't be okay at all.

'I've just been so worried about him and...' Milly started.

'Don't forget about him already,' Uncle Mark said with a wink, putting Joe's lead rope into Milly's hand before her pony walked off.

Milly just giggled. 'I'd let him sleep in my bed if I could, Mr D. There's no way I'll ever forget about him.'

Poppy sighed as her aunt and uncle walked off.

That was the problem, she realised – after everything that had happened, especially with Joe's accident, she was worried they didn't actually know how much the three of them loved their ponies. There was no way Milly had just forgotten to do Joe's back clips up.

'Want to get all our chores done, then go for that ride?' Poppy asked.

'Yes!' Milly was back to her usual self again, her grin back in place. Poppy was relieved after seeing her so miserable for the past few days. 'I'll put him back in his stable and we can finish getting the paddocks cleaned out.'

They put their horses back, grabbed their shovels and started in the front paddock. Poppy pushed poo onto the shovel and filled a wheelbarrow, glancing over and seeing the others were heaving shovel-loads just as fast as she was. She hefted the wheelbarrow up and pushed it to the manure pile, dumping the poo and leaving the wheelbarrow next to it.

'You guys done?' Poppy asked.

She watched as they finished up, then she ran back to the stables with Katie and Milly hot on her heels. Poppy was first back so she turned on the tap and stuck her head under it first, guzzling water before letting the others take a turn.

'Come on, let's go get lunch,' Katie said when she'd had her turn.

'Jam sandwiches?' Poppy asked, wanting to make something fast so they didn't have to stay inside for too long. They walked side by side, across the grass and back to the house.

Casper let out a loud woof as they pulled out everything they needed to make sandwiches. Poppy jumped.

'Casper!' she scolded. 'You scared me.'

'I think he wants the jam,' Katie said, reaching past Poppy and pulling out a jar of peanut butter.

They quickly made sandwiches and Poppy poured three glasses of blackcurrant juice, and then they headed out to the verandah. Poppy didn't want to waste too much time at the house so they could get down for another ride. She'd just sat down in the sun beside Milly, looking out over the paddocks, when Katie walked out.

'That your mobile ringing?' Katie asked. 'I've got mine on me.'

Milly shook her head and Poppy jumped up, recognising the musical ring-tone of her phone.

Sandwich still in her hand, Poppy sprinted down the hall and up the stairs. She dived onto her bed, flopping down when it cut out just as she hit the answer button. Poppy checked the missed calls, worried it was her mum and something was wrong, and then saw it was Sarah. She licked her hand when she felt a plop of jam on her little finger. She was desperate to talk to Sarah but she was only allowed to make calls from her mobile for emergencies. She could try to call her later from the landline, but…

A text message pinged through. Poppy hastily opened Sarah's message.

Sorry for late reply! Just got back. Jessica sounds nasty. Catch her out on camera or something, then they'll have to get rid of her. S xoxo

Poppy grinned and typed a reply, knowing she had plenty of phone credit to be able to send text messages at least.

Milly's horse ok, going to be able to ride him. Good idea. But how can I catch her when we don't know what she'll do next?

Poppy licked at her still-sticky fingers as she waited for another message to come through. It felt like forever before her phone finally pinged.

Set her up. Do something that you know she can't resist, then wait to catch it on your phone.

Poppy lay back on her bed and stared at the white ceiling. Sarah's idea was great. She couldn't believe that none of them had thought of it sooner.

You're the best!

A second later, another message.

Yep, I know :) S xoxo

'Poppy, you up there?' Milly's voice prompted Poppy into action. She bounced up and left her phone on the bed.

'Coming!' she called back to Milly.

Poppy couldn't stop smiling. If Sarah's idea worked and they caught Jessica on camera, then there was no way Aunt Sophie could ignore what she was doing. And then maybe Sophie would finally believe that Jessica was to blame for all the other things going on, too.

'Hey, I have a plan for Jessica,' she announced as she walked back out to the verandah. She reached for her glass of juice and guzzled it, thankful it was still nice and cool.

'What?' Katie asked.

'We need to set up a trap and catch Jessica in the act,' Poppy told them proudly. 'And catch it all on video.'

'You're a genius!' Milly exclaimed.

Poppy grinned. 'Actually, my friend Sarah is.'

'Now I definitely think I'd like her,' Milly said.

'Now we just have to figure out how to catch her out,' Poppy said.

'As much as I want to brainstorm an evil plan, can we go ride? I'm dying to get back on Joe.'

'Brainstorming on horseback,' Katie said with a giggle. 'If only they did that in school, I'd listen way more!'

Poppy laughed as she grabbed her plate and glass to take back into the kitchen.

'Sounds like a plan for making a plan!'

CHAPTER NINE

The Master Plan

'So how exactly are we going to do it?' Katie asked as they rode their horses down one of their favourite trails. 'We kind of need to put a proper plan in place.'

Poppy looked across at her friends and saw Milly lean down and hug Joe. She'd done it a million times already, and Poppy didn't think this would be her last.

'You guys figure it out. I'm no good at plans,' Milly said.

Poppy looked around at the trees, listening to the birds call as she thought out loud. 'It needs to be somewhere we can easily hide and catch her, like in the stables.'

'And a trap she'll easily fall for, but we can't make it too obvious,' Katie added.

'Is there anything leading up to the gymkhana that we could use?' Milly asked. 'We can't wait too long. What if she does something else? To Crystal or Cody this time?'

A shiver ran all the way down Poppy's spine. She couldn't stand the thought of anything happening to Crystal. Or any of the other horses. And it made her even more determined to come up with a good plan as soon as possible, so that they could be rid of Jessica and her meanness.

'Are we plaiting the horses for the gymkhana?' Katie asked.

Poppy shrugged. 'I guess we could, but Aunt Sophie hasn't said we have to.'

'Why? What are you thinking?' Milly asked.

Katie halted, and Poppy and Milly both stopped beside her. 'What if we make a big fuss about wanting Mrs D to help us plait our horses for the gymkhana? Make out we're really excited about it. And we also try really hard to beat the pants off her in practice over the next two days...'

'So she'll be annoyed and want to sabotage all

our hard work?' Poppy asked, liking the way Katie was thinking. It might just work.

'Exactly,' Katie agreed. 'Then we can be hiding in one of the stables to catch her on camera.'

'You reckon it will work?' Poppy asked, her heart starting to pound with excitement.

'I bet it will,' Milly said. 'She's so mean, she won't be able to resist the chance to ruin something else.'

'And if it doesn't?' Katie asked.

Poppy pressed her legs against Crystal and started to walk again, and the other two followed her lead. 'It will,' she said confidently. 'And *if* it doesn't, we'll just have to think of something else.' And hope Jessica doesn't do anything else to our horses in the meantime, she thought with a sigh.

'Well your friend Sarah seems to be have good ideas. If this doesn't work, we'll just have to get her to come up here and help us out,' Milly said, and Poppy noticed her eyes were twinkling with mischief once more. 'Jessica is going *down*!' Milly yelled.

Poppy just laughed. She hoped Milly was right, because there was nothing she'd like more than to show Aunt Sophie and Uncle Mark that her and Milly and Katie weren't to blame for anything that had been going on around Starlight. Not for their horses going without hay, and certainly not for Joe's cover being undone. And then maybe they'd realise that she hadn't been exaggerating about how awful Jessica had been to them, either.

'Great going, girls,' Aunt Sophie called out.

Poppy grinned back at Katie as she rode past. It was like the last few days hadn't even happened. Milly was back in the saddle – with Joe as frisky as ever – and Aunt Sophie seemed happy with how they were all riding.

'Jessica, your turn,' Aunt Sophie called out.

They all watched as Jessica attempted the course for the second time. They'd all done well the first time, but Katie had beaten them hands down. She was always so careful, guiding Cody calmly around the course without knocking any rails, and now she'd figured out how to go faster. Poppy doubted she'd be able to beat Katie ever again.

Cleopatra lifted her knees high over every

fence, making the course look easy, and she happily cantered, cruising fast around the show jumps. Poppy sighed as she watched – Jessica's horse always looked amazing. But Jessica didn't look happy, and she still insisted on giving Cleopatra a few smacks with her whip, like she was scared she was going to stop instead of jump. Poppy cringed, wishing she could grab the crop and give Jessica a whack with it so she knew what it felt like!

'Good work, Jessica,' Aunt Sophie praised. 'I'd like to see you ride without a whip next time, though. You need to trust that she'll look after you, and not try to rush her.'

Poppy stifled a laugh. It was like Sophie had read her mind!

Jessica pouted, but Aunt Sophie just shook her head. 'None of the other girls need to ride with one, and Cleopatra's the most talented jumper here. No offence to your ponies, girls,' she said with a smile.

'Aunt Sophie,' Poppy called, getting her aunt's attention. 'Would it be okay if we practised plaiting for the gymkhana with you?'

'That would be way cool,' Milly chimed in. Poppy grinned at her.

'You don't have to plait horses for Pony Club gymkhanas,' Aunt Sophie said.

Poppy glanced at her friends. She hadn't thought that Sophie could be the one to muck up their plans. 'They look so pretty, though, don't you think?' she said sweetly.

'Is it okay if we do?' asked Katie. 'I'd love to see Cody all plaited up. And then we can practise what you've shown us. I bet they'll all look so cool.'

Aunt Sophie looked pleased. 'That's a great idea, girls. Jessica, do you want to plait Cleopatra?'

Jessica shook her head. 'No. Don't you have a groom that can do it?'

Poppy and Milly both groaned at the same time. Seriously, this girl just kept getting more annoying!

'If you'd like to join in, I'd love to show you how,' Aunt Sophie said, completely ignoring what she'd asked. 'She'd look beautiful all plaited up.'

'No thanks,' Jessica said.

Poppy, Katie and Milly exchanged looks, all smiling. Everything was going perfectly to plan. They just had to hope that the rest of the plan went as smoothly, and Jessica didn't do anything else to their horses before they caught her out.

The gymkhana was only two days away, and so they'd be plaiting up the following night ready for the day ahead. It felt like they'd only just gotten back to Starlight Stables after their time at home, and now it was already time for their first real competition. Poppy tried not to think about how few days they had left. She had her own pony now, which meant she was going to be coming to Starlight more than ever, visiting every second weekend. But the thought of not seeing Milly and Katie for weeks at a time when she was back home in Melbourne made her sad.

'Come on, girls. I want you to practise barrel racing for me before you take the horses for a nice long walk. Let's go!'

Poppy made a clucking sound and gave Crystal a little kick, laughing as Crystal burst into a canter and they left the others behind. Milly hated not being first, and Poppy knew it!

'Slow down!' Aunt Sophie called.

Poppy did as she was told, slowing to a trot. 'Can I go first?' she yelled back.

'Go for it,' Aunt Sophie said.

Poppy burst into a canter again and raced toward the first barrel. She might not be able to beat Katie at show jumping, but she wasn't going to let her friend come first when it came to games. Crystal was fast, and Poppy wasn't going to hold her back.

They raced toward the first barrel. Poppy leaned forward, urging Crystal on. Without slowing, Crystal spun around the barrel, digging her hooves into the dirt and almost slicing Poppy's knee off they were so close to the metal. They cantered fast toward the next barrel. Crystal looped around it and raced to the final one before galloping to the finish line.

Poppy couldn't wipe the grin off her face as she passed her friends. Even Jessica's sullen stare wasn't enough to stop her feeling awesome.

'Beat that, Mils!' she joked.

Milly poked out her tongue. 'You betcha.'

Joe burst away from the others, head high as he raced to the first barrel. He didn't turn as fast as Crystal, overshooting the barrel instead of sticking close to it, but he was so quick Poppy doubted it mattered. If they had been timed, Poppy bet it would be close between them.

By the time they'd all done their practice rounds, the horses were hot and sweaty – but Crystal was raring to go again.

'Okay, now I'm timing each of you,' Aunt Sophie said. 'Poppy, you can start. Ready… Go!'

Poppy was as excited as Crystal as she clamped her legs and Crystal shot off to race around the barrels for a second time.

'Go, Pops!' Katie and Milly yelled.

Aunt Sophie laughed when Poppy came galloping back past her. '19 seconds. Great work!'

Poppy gave Crystal a big pat on the neck 'Extra sugar cubes for you!' she promised.

Milly was only a second slower than Poppy, and the other two didn't come close, so Poppy was super proud of herself and Crystal.

'Let them stretch their legs, girls, then hose them down, put their rugs on and turn them out for the night.'

They were all out of breath still, and Poppy was happy to take Crystal for a walk.

'You did great around the jumps, Jessica,' Poppy said, forcing herself to be nice while her aunt was listening. 'Cleopatra is amazing.'

Jessica sat up straight and smiled. 'Thanks. She is pretty incredible. She's just better at jumping than silly games.'

Milly made a face like she was going to vomit, but Poppy ignored her. 'Are you sure you don't want to plait her up? We could all do it together.'

'No thanks,' Jessica said with a grimace. 'I'd rather go home than hang around the stables longer than I have to.'

Poppy almost felt sorry for her. She wondered if Jessica even liked horses that much. Poppy would do anything to spend every minute of her life around horses. Jessica had the most amazing horse and a mum who wanted her to ride, and yet she couldn't wait to leave the stables and Cleopatra. Poppy couldn't help but think how sad that was.

'I can't wait,' Katie said, rubbing her hand back and forth down her horse's neck. 'Cody will look amazing.'

'I bet they'll all have ribbons around their necks on the day, and they'll look so cool if they're all plaited,' Milly added.

Poppy frowned, wondering if they were making too big a deal out of it. Would Jessica be suspicious? She didn't want Jessica to be mean, but she did want to catch her in the act so that they could clear their names to Aunt Sophie.

'Well, we'll be down at the stables plaiting after lessons tomorrow. We have to be in for dinner by seven,' Poppy told her. 'If you change your mind, come down.'

'I won't,' Jessica insisted, turning Cleopatra around and heading back toward the stables.

'Aren't you going to stretch her out?' Poppy asked.

Jessica shrugged. 'I hate riding around the farm. I thought I told you that already.'

Poppy didn't even bother saying that Aunt Sophie would be disappointed with her for not cooling her horse down properly, because she knew she wouldn't listen anyway. Poppy hated the way Jessica mistreated Cleopatra, but she just had to hope that, eventually, Aunt Sophie would see what her new riding pupil was really like.

'I reckon she's scared of riding anywhere but in the arena,' Milly said.

'No, I think she just doesn't like riding all that much,' Katie disagreed. 'There's something funny about the way she is with her horse. I bet she doesn't even want to ride.'

Poppy didn't know what to make of Jessica,

116

but she did know that she didn't like her. She was mean to them and her horse, and there was nothing nice about her. The quicker they caught her in the act, the better, and then they could just have fun and enjoy the gymkhana. All they had to do was sneak out of the house after dinner tomorrow and wait, and hope like crazy that she actually did try to sabotage their plaiting. If she didn't, Poppy was all out of ideas. And then they might be stuck with Jessica riding at Starlight forever.

CHAPTER TEN

Gymkhana Eve

The day was hot and the wind whipped up the dirt into clouds around Poppy, Milly and Katie. Poppy rubbed her eyes and trudged up to the house. Her legs ached, her arms were sore from cleaning out water troughs and lugging hay bales, and all she wanted to do was get in the shower and scrub her skin.

'Wait up!' Milly called out.

Poppy turned and held up her hand to shield her eyes. The sun was still bright even though it was late afternoon.

'I bags the shower first,' Poppy declared.

'Then I'm second,' Milly grumbled. 'I'm so

tired, I think I'm gonna drop dead.'

Poppy smiled and they leaned against each other as they walked.

'Was that mean of me to say?'

Poppy frowned. 'What?'

'Making jokes about me dropping dead. You know, after your dad, you know.'

'It's fine,' Poppy said, feeling touched by her friend's sensitivity. She slung her arm around Milly's shoulders. 'I mean, I still don't like to think about what happened, but you don't have to worry about saying things around me. Honest.'

Milly looked at her as if she wasn't sure whether to believe her or not. But the truth was, Poppy *was* feeling better about things. When they were back home last week, Sophie had sat her down with her mum so they could talk, and Poppy knew she would be eternally grateful to Sophie who somehow knew all the right questions to ask and things to say to make her mum really open up.

They had all spoken to the counsellor, too, and Poppy was thankful that they were treating her like an adult, explaining everything to her so she understood the therapy process her mum was going through, instead of hiding what was really going on behind kind, sympathetic faces, like they were still doing with her brother. Now, Poppy felt like she could chat to her mum honestly, and ask her all the questions that she'd been too afraid to ask when Mum was in her bad phase. And she felt that she could talk about her dad now – the counsellor had helped her untangle all her feelings so that her grief for her dad was no longer mixed up with her worry for her mum. She did still miss her dad all the time, but she didn't feel like crying much now, and she was able to think about all the fun times she'd had with him again.

Poppy smiled as she remembered all the conversations with her dad on the phone, when he was serving overseas as a soldier, and how she'd always rattle on about her latest trip to Starlight and every time, he'd ask her, 'Anything to report that doesn't involve horses, Popster?'.

Katie caught up to them and raced ahead, reaching the house door first and snapping Poppy out of her thoughts. 'Shower's mine,' Katie said.

'No!' Poppy yelled at her, stumbling as she kicked her boots off before launching down the hall toward the stairs to get to the bathroom. 'I bagsed it first!'

'What's the hurry, girls?' Sophie asked, coming out of the living room.

They all skidded on the timber floor in their socks, banging together and giggling.

'Shower,' Milly explained, out of breath and between giggles. 'Poppy put first dibs on it, but Katie beat her and I was just trying to catch up.'

Aunt Sophie smiled and touched Poppy's shoulder. 'How about you girls clean up and then meet me down at the stables. We'll plait the ponies before dinner, and then you can all have an early night so that you're fresh for the gymkhana tomorrow.'

Poppy's heart started to beat fast again just thinking about the gymkhana. They'd been so busy putting their plan together to catch Jessica out, on top of doing their chores and riding and practising, that she'd hardly had time to even think about the gymkhana. But now it was almost time... she gulped. Her stomach was all jumpy – she felt a bit sick with nerves. She'd been looking forward to competing at a Pony Club gymkhana since she'd first starting riding!

'Is Jessica going to meet us there in the morning?' Milly asked. She sounded so innocent – Poppy didn't know how she did it. Poppy always went bright red when she was up to something, and gave herself away before she'd even said anything.

'Her mum's going to drive her here first thing, then they'll follow our truck to the Pony Club grounds.' Aunt Sophie turned to walk away then looked over her shoulder at them. 'I'm really proud of you girls, the way you've been training and listening to my instructions. You're going to do great tomorrow.'

Poppy's smile stretched across her entire face. All she ever wanted was to make her aunt proud, so it meant a lot to her hearing her say that.

'Thanks, Mrs D,' Katie said first.

Milly threw her arms around Aunt Sophie and gave her a tight hug, and Poppy just kept grinning.

'I'll take some snacks down to the stables, so just get yourselves showered and meet me there,' Aunt Sophie said, while untangling herself from Milly.

Poppy saw her chance. She elbowed Katie out of the way and sprinted upstairs and into the bathroom, slamming the door behind her.

'Poppy!' Katie shrieked.

'I'll only be a sec,' she said with a giggle, turning on the water then tugging her hair from its plait and stripping her clothes off.

'I think we'll start calling you Jessica,' Milly called out from the other side of the door.

'Don't you dare!' Poppy yelled back, jumping under the hot water and opening her mouth to catch some. The powerful stream felt good and soothed her sore muscles. She reminded herself to be quick, though, washing her hair then drying off and wrapping herself in a big fluffy towel before opening the door to let one of the others in. They were slumped against the wall, half asleep.

'Who's next?'

Milly was up first and Katie moaned. 'Seriously?'

'Hey,' Poppy said, 'you're gonna beat the pants off us tomorrow, so don't feel bad about us getting to the shower first. Cody will be covered in ribbons.'

Katie's smile was shy. 'You really think so?'

'I know so,' Poppy told her, twirling her wet hair between her fingers. 'So long as you beat Jessica, I'll be happy.'

'Thanks, Pop.'

Poppy left her waiting in the hall, and went to their room to change. As she ran the comb through her tangled hair, she hoped that she'd be good enough to beat both of her friends. She knew Katie would do well, so she wasn't lying – she just hoped Crystal would do better than Cody. But as long as Katie beat Jessica, then she'd still be smiling.

Plaiting Crystal was a lot harder than Poppy had thought it was going to be. Aunt Sophie had started each of them off, and she was still coming back and forth to help, but Poppy's fingers were numb from making so many tiny plaits along Crystal's mane. She had one tiny plait left to go, then they had to twist each plait into a tiny ball to make it look like a little rosette, and finally secure it with a small rubber band. It was a long process.

When Aunt Sophie was preparing for a dressage competition, Poppy had seen her use a needle and thread to sew hers perfectly, which she thought looked crazy hard.

'I'm going to do their tails for you,' Aunt Sophie announced as she came out of the tack shed. 'Then we can head back for dinner and you can all have that early night.'

Poppy blew out a breath, and a loose hair that had escaped her ponytail tickled her nose. She twisted a plait into a ball, like Aunt Sophie had showed her, and secured it. It's not perfect, but it still looks pretty good, she thought proudly as she tucked the loose hair behind her ear and itched her nose.

'How you guys going?' Poppy asked the others.

All three ponies were cross-tied outside their stables, and the girls were standing on overturned wooden crates that had been lying around the stables. It made plaiting the manes a whole lot easier, rather than getting aching arms from trying to reach up high.

'I'm almost hoping she doesn't try to ruin them,' Katie muttered when Aunt Sophie disappeared into the tack shed. 'I don't want to do this all over again in the morning.'

'In the morning?' Milly squeaked. 'I don't want to do this ever again.'

Katie and Poppy laughed at her. 'I think it gets easier the more practice you get,' Poppy told her.

'Practice shmactice,' Milly moaned. 'This sucks.'

'What sucks?' Aunt Sophie was laughing as she spoke.

'Nothing,' Milly said quickly.

'I don't think we realised how hard it would be to actually plait an entire mane,' Katie confessed.

Poppy laughed. She'd always known it was going to be tough, but Katie was right.

'It'll be worth it in the morning when you saddle up and see how gorgeous they look,' Sophie said. 'I bet even Tom will be impressed.'

Poppy looked up at the mention of her brother. 'I'm such a doofus,' she said.

'Why?' Katie asked.

Poppy went back to twisting the little plaits, annoyed at herself for forgetting. 'My brother arrives here tomorrow,' she said. 'But I'd forgotten about it with everything that's been going on, and preparing for the gymkhana.'

Poppy was looking forward to seeing Tom. Before her dad had died, she'd spent half her life thinking her brother was a pain, but things were different now. They'd been through a lot together, and she felt protective of him now in a way that she never had before. She hoped he would have a fun time with the kids here at pony camp that were his age.

Aunt Sophie smiled then looked away, still grinning, and Poppy narrowed her eyes. Something was up.

'You're looking at me all funny,' she accused her aunt.

'I'm not.'

Milly and Katie stopped what they were doing and stared at Aunt Sophie, too.

'Yeah, you are,' Milly confirmed.

'Yep, something's up,' Katie said.

Aunt Sophie threw her hands up in the air. 'You girls! Talk about a way to ruin a surprise.'

'What surprise?!' Poppy demanded. She dropped the plait she'd been working on, staring at her aunt.

'You'll just have to wait and see,' Aunt Sophie said.

Poppy couldn't wipe the grin off her face, and caught herself before she fell off the crate she was standing on. 'Please!' Poppy begged. She had no clue what it could be, although she wasn't sure anything could top her aunt's last surprise for her, when she gave her Crystal.

'Just look forward to seeing Tom, okay?' Sophie said. 'He can't wait to get here.'

'I wish Sarah was coming with him,' Katie said. 'It'd be so cool to meet her.'

'Ohmygod, is it Sarah?' Poppy asked. 'Is she coming here?' She'd been begging her to come for years!

'No sweetheart, it's not. Now just get back to plaiting.'

'Yeah, it'd be great to meet the mastermind plan genius,' Milly said.

Poppy dropped what she was doing again and gave Milly a wide-eyed look. She saw Katie roll her eyes, too. As soon as the words were out, Poppy saw the realisation dawn on Milly's face that she'd just dropped them in it with Sophie.

'Mastermind plan?' Aunt Sophie asked, not missing anything. 'What are you talking about?'

'Ummmm…' Milly mumbled.

'Sarah suggested to Poppy that the horses might do even better on the day if they looked all beautiful,' Katie interrupted, saving the day again.

'But I thought it was Milly's idea to do this,' Aunt Sophie said, her eyebrows drawn together like she knew something was up and was trying to figure them out.

'I, ah, told Milly what Sarah said. She thought it was a good idea and was just, well, excited about doing the horses up for the gymkhana I guess,' Poppy said, thinking quick so they didn't end up having to spill the beans. She felt her face going red, and hoped Sophie didn't notice.

Aunt Sophie shrugged, seeming convinced. Poppy watched as her aunt started on Cody's tail now she'd finished Crystal's, making quick work of the intricate reverse French plait. Poppy blew out a sigh of relief and exchanged glances with the other two. They looked as freaked out as she felt.

But thinking about Tom had given her an idea. She knew her mum had packed a bag for Tom and given it to Sophie to bring up in the car, thinking it would be easier than him having to bring it on the train. And Poppy bet Tom would have put his walkie-talkies in there – he'd always loved using them around the farm at Starlight – and if they used his walkie-talkies for their Jessica plan, then they'd be able to hide separately and still communicate, which meant it would be so much easier to catch Jessica out!

Poppy was desperate to tell Milly and Katie about her idea, so she finished Crystal's mane as quickly as she could and then put her special silky combo cover on that would make her pony's coat all shiny, before letting her into the stable. She checked Crystal's hay and water, and then rushed out to do the same for her friends, checking that both their stables were ready for the evening.

When she came back out of Cody's box, Katie gave her a puzzled look, but Poppy just winked at her – she'd tell them her plan when they were walking back to the house, safe out of Sophie's earshot.

Aunt Sophie gave Cody a pat on the bottom and moved across to Joe, pausing to check their manes first.

'As soon as you've finished Cody's mane, Katie, put his rug on and then you can all three head back to the house for dinner. Milly, I'll finish off Joe's tail, and then sort him out for the night,' she told them. 'Mark should have dinner ready by now, and I want you all to get an early night so you're fresh for tomorrow.'

Poppy helped Katie throw Cody's cover on, and buckled up the back straps for her while Katie did the front. Milly had finished Joe's plaits, too, and Poppy shooed her and Katie out of the stable.

'What's the big rush?' Katie asked.

'I've had an idea,' Poppy said.

Milly groaned. 'Did that hurt your head?'

'Ha ha, very funny,' Poppy muttered.

'Well, what is it?' Katie asked again.

'When we were talking about Tom before, I remembered that Sophie brought his bag in the car with us, and I'll bet you anything that his walkie-talkies are in there,' Poppy said. 'I thought we could use them tonight for, you know, catching Jessica. One of us can be lookout with one walkie-talkie, and use it to alert whoever's in the stable that Jessica's coming, and whether her mum is with her or not.'

'That's banking on the fact that she'll come back,' Katie said. 'I'm starting to worry that she won't even do it. I mean, what if she wants to sabotage the plaits but her mum won't drive her back tonight. I can't see Jessica riding a bike!'

Poppy laughed. 'Yeah, I know, but it was the only plan we came up with, right? We just have to cross our fingers that it does work.'

'I reckon we should hide in the stable they use

for hay. It would be a good spot to watch everything from, and she wouldn't be able to see us,' Katie said.

'Sounds good,' Poppy agreed.

'She's going to do it,' Milly insisted. 'I just know she will. And I reckon the walkie talkie idea is perfect. Whoever's on lookout can race back to the house and get Mrs D as soon as we have the evidence.'

It was just starting to get dark. Poppy loved the long summer days – more hours of daylight meant more time to ride. But right now, all Poppy wanted to do was eat. She was so hungry, her tummy was making very funny noises. The snacks that Sophie had brought down to the stables had done nothing to take the edge off Poppy's hunger.

'Mark's cooking,' Poppy said with a giggle. 'What do you think it'll be?'

'Hmmm, it wouldn't be his world-famous spaghetti, would it?' Milly joked back.

They were all laughing as they burst through the door, the smell of Mark's Italian cooking making Poppy's stomach growl even louder.

'Wash your hands and meet me at the table girls,' Uncle Mark called out. 'It's ready and waiting.'

They all kicked off their boots at the door and

made their way into the bathroom off the hall to wash their hands. Poppy was nervous, thinking about everything that could go wrong with their plan tonight. If Sophie and Mark caught them in the stables and they had no Jessica evidence, Poppy knew they could just say they were too excited to sleep and wanted to be with their horses. Aunt Sophie wouldn't be too angry about that, she figured, except about their sneaking out when they were supposed to be in bed. But still, Poppy was worried. She hated making Sophie angry, and the last thing she wanted was for them to all get in trouble. Again.

'I knew it! Here they are,' Poppy said, pulling the walkie-talkies out of Tom's bag. She zipped the bag closed again and crept back across the landing. Milly and Katie were waiting in their beds, wide awake and fully clothed, ready to sneak out once Sophie and Mark were settled watching TV.

'Is Mrs D going to kill us for sneaking out?' Katie asked.

Milly shook her head. 'She won't catch us. And

when we tell her what's happened, she'll forget all about the fact that we weren't supposed to be down there.'

Poppy gulped. She hoped Milly was right. She passed one of the handsets to Katie and walked out to the hall, pressing the button on hers to see if it was working. 'Over and out,' she whispered.

Katie laughed. 'Roger that!'

'So they're working,' Poppy said, walking back in to their room. 'How long should we wait before heading down to the stables? It sounds like the TV's on downstairs, so Sophie and Mark will have their backs to the door – we'll just have to be super quiet.'

'I reckon we should go down now. Imagine if Jessica's already done it and we missed the whole thing,' Milly said. Poppy could tell that Milly was impatient for the adventure to begin, but she knew she was right – they didn't know when Jessica might turn up, so the sooner they got down there, the better.

'So, who's on lookout?' Katie asked.

Poppy shrugged and held out her hand for rock, paper, scissors. 'Loser has to be lookout?' she suggested. 'The other two get to be in the barn to catch her.'

'One, two, three, go!' Poppy said, as they each revealed their hands from behind their backs. Milly cheered when her rock beat both Katie and Poppy's scissors, and grabbed one of the walkie-talkies off the bed.

Poppy took a deep breath. Katie's eyes were locked on hers. Poppy knew neither of them wanted to be lookout. She decided to go with scissors again, but then changed her mind at the last minute and punched the air when her paper covered Katie's rock.

'Sorry,' Poppy said, immediately feeling bad for Katie.

'I don't mind,' Katie said, and shrugged like she really truly didn't care as she picked up the other walkie-talkie. 'I'd rather keep an eye out than be the one to confront her.'

'So this is it,' Poppy said, her voice shaky, betraying her nervousness.

'Yep.' Milly looked around the room. 'Let's stuff our pillows into the beds so it looks like we're in there asleep if Mrs D checks.'

Poppy went along with it, but she doubted it would fool Aunt Sophie. She always checked them properly before she went to bed herself. But then again, it was super early, way earlier than they ever usually went to bed, so she probably wouldn't come up before they were back. She grabbed her phone, making sure it was fully charged, so they could catch Jessica on video. She just hoped their plan worked, otherwise they could be in a power-load of trouble.

CHAPTER ELEVEN

The Plan

'I'm scared it's all going to go wrong,' Katie said. She was rubbing her hands up and down her arms like she was super cold.

Poppy passed her the hoodie she'd brought down. 'Here. You're the one who's going to be out here. Put this on.'

'Thanks.'

'And don't be scared. Just radio us as soon as you see her, or if there's any sign of Aunt Sophie or Uncle Mark, okay?' Poppy was scared of their plan not working, too, she just didn't want to say so.

Poppy and Milly left Katie hidden behind a tree at the curve in the driveway, so she could see both up and down it. They ran down to the stables, going straight through the side door and looking in on all three ponies to make sure they were still all plaited up. They were, and were just munching their hay, blinking at the girls as they watched them.

'So far so good. Let's go find a good hiding spot,' Milly said.

Poppy headed for the hay storage stall, then stopped. 'Uh-oh, looks like Sophie filled it with more hay. We're going to have to find somewhere else.'

'How about the stable across from Crystal and Joe? We can hide with whatever horse is in there?' Milly suggested.

Poppy grinned. 'Perfect.' It was probably the best spot anyway, because they'd have a perfect view of all their ponies.

They let themselves in to one of the riding school horses' stable. Sophie had kept him in along with a few others, because some of the older riding school pupils were competing tomorrow, and would meet them at the Pony Club grounds in the morning.

'Hey, Missy,' Poppy said, scratching the sweet grey mare as she came over to see what they were doing. 'We're just going to hang out with you for a while.' Poppy laughed as Missy nuzzled her bare arm. Missy was one of her old favourites at Starlight. She'd ridden her most holidays when she came to visit, before she had Crystal, and she felt guilty she hadn't been hanging out with her more this holiday. She'd been leased out to a local rider for a while, and Poppy hoped she'd had fun while she'd been away.

'So what now?' Milly asked.

Poppy shrugged. 'We wait, I guess.' She pulled out two chupa-chups and passed one to Milly. 'I guess she'd want to do it while it's still light. Which can't be too much longer...'

It felt like hours had passed by the time Poppy was twirling her chupa-chup in her mouth with nothing left on the stick. She sighed and leaned back against Missy. Her eyes were starting to get heavy. She could have done with that early night. She taunted herself, thinking about her comfy bed. She looked over at Milly's watch. She couldn't believe it – they'd only been here half an hour.

'Want to radio Katie?' Poppy asked.

Milly was slumped over the stable door, watching Joe. 'Yeah.' She pulled the walkie-talkie out of her pocket. 'Katie, you there?'

The walkie-talkie screeched and made Missy jump. Poppy quickly reached out to comfort her, stroking her neck.

'I'm here. Nothing to report.' Katie replied.

'I'm so tired,' Milly moaned.

'Scrap that! Guys, she's here! You hear me?'

Poppy felt her heart beat faster in her chest. This was it. She grabbed the walkie-talkie from Milly and replied to Katie. 'You sure it's her?'

'Black Range Rover, going slow across the gravel. Heading straight for the stables.'

'Don't radio again in case she hears. We'll tell you when we've got what we need.'

Poppy dropped the walkie-talkie into the sawdust because her hands were all fumbly, her palms damp. She couldn't believe it. Jessica had taken the bait, and this was actually happening.

Poppy wiped her hands on her jeans and pulled her phone from her pocket, ready to catch Jessica on video. Milly was staring at her. Her eyes were wide but a cheeky smile played on her lips. Poppy knew she was thinking the same thing. Their plan was working!

'Silent as a mouse,' Poppy whispered to her.

Milly nodded and they stood side by side, shoulders hard together. They ducked down a little so Jessica wouldn't see them when she passed Missy's stall. Poppy listened for Jessica's footsteps. She checked her phone was on video mode, and waited...

CHAPTER TWELVE

Caught!

Poppy's breath was coming in short bursts. She was trying so hard to be quiet, but her heart was hammering in her chest, and she felt sure that Jessica would hear it. A car door slammed and Poppy jumped. Jessica was here!

'She's coming,' Milly whispered, ducking down lower, grabbing hold of Poppy's hand.

A squeak echoed out, which Poppy recognised as the door to the stables, and there was a soft thud of boots on the concrete floor. Poppy stayed stock still, and Milly looked like she was holding her breath next to her.

Once she was certain Jessica had gone past,

Poppy nudged Milly then crept up to peek over the stall door. She hit record on her phone. Poppy couldn't see Jessica, but she could hear her rustling in the tack room. She pointed the camera at the tack room door.

Jessica appeared with a bucket. Poppy felt herself go bug-eyed as she watched Jessica slip silently into Crystal's stall. Poppy felt sick, torn between wanting to stop her doing anything to Crystal and catching her out to stop her once and for all.

Her heart was racing even faster now, and her hands were slippery from nervous sweat, but she held the phone as steady as she could, double-checking again to make sure the red dot was flashing to say it was recording.

Yes! She was getting it all on video. She watched Jessica make fast work of Crystal's plaits. She looked like she was in a serious hurry. She wondered what she'd told her mum to get her to bring her back.

Milly was still sat on the floor of Missy's stall, looking like she was hyperventilating, so Poppy nudged Milly with her foot and gestured for her to wriggle up next to her.

'What's she feeding her?' Poppy mouthed.

Milly frowned, wriggling closer to Poppy as they both peered over.

Poppy tried to keep her hand still but her arm was aching from holding it up for so long. Through the phone's screen, Poppy watched Jessica give one last tug and pull the pretty braid from Crystal's forelock. It burst out all cute and curly, but Poppy's heart dropped to see all her hard work ruined like that. Poppy went to grab Milly's hand as she watched, but Milly was already heaving Missy's stall door open before Poppy could stop her.

'How dare you!' Milly yelled, bursting out of the stall and marching straight toward Jessica. 'I knew you were the one who'd tried to hurt Joe!'

Poppy was feeling jittery as she hit the button on her screen to stop recording, and then dropped the phone when she fumbled for the walkie-talkie. She panicked and scrambled through the hay for the phone. She couldn't lose the video! She quickly checked the video was saved, slipped the phone into her pocket and radioed Katie.

'Katie! Get Sophie, now!'

Katie answered back straightaway. 'I'm running!'

Poppy let herself out of the stall, securing it

again quickly so Missy couldn't escape. Poppy could see she was jittery, too, with all the excitement going on around her. As she turned around, she almost slammed straight into Jessica who was trying to run past Milly.

'You're dead!' Milly yelled, grabbing hold of Jessica's arm. 'You hurt Joe, you tried to starve all our horses, and now look what you've done to Crystal!'

Poppy leapt into action, not about to let Jessica go running off before Aunt Sophie came down.

'You're not getting away with it this time,' Poppy said, grabbing Jessica's other arm and gripping tight.

'Let go of me!' Jessica yelled.

'Wait until Mrs D finds out what you've done,' Milly said triumphantly. 'You'll never be welcome here again.'

Jessica was still struggling to get away, and Poppy could only just keep hold of her.

'She'll never believe you,' Jessica sneered. 'Why would she believe you over me?'

Poppy and Milly exchanged glances and laughed. 'She will when she sees the video,' Poppy told her.

'What video?' Jessica suddenly looked scared.

Her lower lip visibly trembled.

Poppy almost felt bad. Jessica looked like she was about to cry, but then she glanced over at her pony and saw all her hard work ruined – the only trace of the plaits was Crystal's curly tangle of mane – which made Poppy all the more determined to make sure Jessica was punished for what she'd done.

'Did you really think you were going to get away with all the mean things you've been doing?' Milly asked.

Jessica did start to cry then. Big tears fell in plops down her cheeks, and Poppy didn't know whether she was just really good at pretending or if she was actually feeling bad.

'Please don't tell Sophie. Don't let her see the video,' Jessica begged.

Poppy let go of her arm a little. Were they doing the right thing? she worried. She gulped down the doubt. *They* hadn't done anything wrong, *Jessica* had.

The walkie-talkie crackled. Poppy fished it from the band of her jods, keeping hold of Jessica with her other hand.

'Sophie's coming, but she told me I had to stay

at the house,' Katie told them.

Poppy paused before answering. 'Was she mad?'

There was nothing but static for a second. Then, 'Yeah.'

Jessica's eyes looked like they were going to pop out of her head. She stared at Poppy. Her eyes seemed to be pleading. Poppy loosened her grip on Jessica's arm, but noticed Milly was still holding on tight to Jessica's other arm.

'My mum will kill me. She's out in the car now,' Jessica said.

'We know,' Poppy said. 'Katie was keeping look out when you arrived.'

'But you don't understand what she's like. Please,' Jessica begged. 'I don't even like horses, or riding. My mum's made me do it since I was four because it was what *she* wanted. She's making me do it because she always wanted a horse. But I hate it. I hate it.'

Poppy did feel sorry for her then. She took a step back, loosening her hold on her. 'You don't even like horses?' That was the bit she couldn't believe. But then it did kind of make sense, the way she was with Cleopatra.

'I'm always begging her to let me stop riding, but she just keeps telling me that I have to win. That I have to be the best. That I have to ride.' Jessica was sobbing now. 'I just wanted to make sure I was going to win. I keep thinking that if I win everything, if I make her happy because I win every class, that she might finally stop pushing me because I've done everything she wants.' She cried even louder. 'I just hate it!'

'Girls? What's going on down here?' Aunt Sophie called out, rushing toward them. 'Jessica, what are you doing here?'

Poppy hated that they'd worried Aunt Sophie again. It was the second time they'd caused trouble at Starlight Stables, but this had been the only way to show her how awful Jessica was.

'Look what she did to Crystal,' Milly said, pointing toward Crystal's stable. 'We caught it all on video.'

Poppy watched Aunt Sophie's face go through the emotions, from anger to questioning disbelief. Her eyes fell on Poppy, and Poppy nodded at her, hoping she'd understand.

'I'm sorry, Aunt Sophie, but we wanted to prove

to you what she was really like.'

'But, how did you know I was–' Jessica started, but Aunt Sophie cut her off.

'Jessica, is this true?' Aunt Sophie never took her eyes from Jessica until the girl finally hung her head and nodded.

'I did it,' she confessed. 'But please don't tell my mum. Please. Just let me go and I promise never to do anything else again. You can punish me all you like here, just don't tell her.'

Aunt Sophie crossed over to Crystal to inspect her mane. 'Oh my goodness. Jessica! How could you do this? Poppy worked on those plaits for hours.' They watched as Sophie stepped into the stable, gasping less than a second later. 'Jessica! Did you give Crystal this entire bucket of oats?'

Poppy pushed Jessica out of the way to get to Crystal, running the few steps and bursting in behind Aunt Sophie. Why didn't she check the bucket Jessica had been carrying? She'd been so desperate to catch her out that she'd forgotten all about it!

'Will she be okay?' Poppy asked, tears welling in her eyes now.

149

'I don't know,' Aunt Sophie said, removing the bucket and running a hand over Crystal's shoulder. 'How full was the bucket, Jessica?'

Jessica wasn't saying anything. She was still staring at her boots.

'Jessica?'

'Almost full,' Jessica mumbled.

'Poppy, go with Milly and tell Mark to come down here immediately.'

'Why?' Poppy's hand had started to shake.

'Because she could well end up with a belly ache or, even worse, colic.' Sophie ran a hand over Crystal's back. 'She's only ever had a handful of oats before, and always with chaff or other roughage. Just eating a massive amount of oats on their own like this could cause her a whole lot of trouble.'

Colic? It was the only word circling in Poppy's head. Poppy knew horses died of that all the time. She'd heard her aunt and uncle talk about it lots.

'Can't I stay with her? Please, Aunt Sophie,' she begged. 'Don't make me go.'

'What I need you to do is get Mark right now,' Aunt Sophie said, her voice firm but calm. 'And I want you girls to stay in the house until I come for you. No sneaking out.' She sighed, stepping out of the stable. 'Leave the phone here so I can watch the video, and Jessica, go and get your mother. Now.'

Poppy grabbed Milly's hand and they walked quickly out of the stables, even though Poppy's legs felt like jelly they were so wobbly. Neither of them said a word. She'd watched Jessica disappear into the feed room and take the bucket in, but she'd guessed it was just some feed to make Crystal stand still while she pulled the plaits out, not that she'd try to give her so much grain that she could hurt her.

Please don't let Crystal die. Please don't let Crystal die, Poppy silently begged. She grabbed Milly's hand and started to run. She couldn't lose Crystal. She just couldn't.

CHAPTER THIRTEEN

Crystal

If her heart was capable of breaking, Poppy was sure it would be in hundreds and thousands of tiny pieces. She was huddled beneath the doona with Katie and Milly on either side of her, all squished into her bed. None of them were saying anything. They hadn't spoken a word since Poppy had told Uncle Mark to get down to the stable as quickly as he could.

'I need to go down there,' Poppy said, her voice still all wobbly and weird.

'She said not to,' Milly said. 'I think we should wait.'

Poppy shut her eyes tight. Milly never told her to do anything sensible, but if even she thought she should stay put...? Poppy sighed and cuddled the doona tighter.

'Did you hear that?' Katie whispered.

Poppy sat bolt upright. 'Was it the door?'

They all sat, silent, listening. Footsteps echoed on the timber floor downstairs, then Poppy heard the familiar sound of Aunt Sophie taking off her boots. She wanted to run to her, but she was also scared. Scared of finding out about Crystal, of hearing bad news.

'Girls?' Aunt Sophie called out. Poppy could hear her soft footsteps walking across the lounge to the foot of the stairs. 'Are you up there?'

Before they could all untangle themselves from the doona, Aunt Sophie was standing in the doorway. She smiled and crossed the room, sitting down on the bed with them.

'I feel like I should be telling you off for sneaking out on me. Again,' she said, referring to the times they'd snuck down to the barn to protect their ponies from the horse thief. Poppy looked at her aunt. She seemed tired and weary, she thought, and Poppy was sorry to think she'd caused it. 'But what you did tonight took courage.'

Poppy looked at Milly and Katie. Milly was bursting with triumph.

'We knew she'd been the one doing things to our horses,' Milly said.

Aunt Sophie held up her hand, and Milly shut up. 'I should have trusted you all more and believed you,' Sophie continued. 'Jessica confessed to stealing your horses' hay and undoing Joe's back straps on his cover that day. Not to mention what she did tonight.'

Poppy didn't care about all of that. She didn't care about getting in trouble or even what Jessica had done. All she cared about was Crystal and making sure she was okay.

'Is she going to die?' Poppy asked, biting down hard on her lip to stop the tears. She would never forgive Jessica for this. Never.

'Who? Crystal?' Aunt Sophie asked.

Poppy closed her eyes and felt Sophie's arm around her. This is it, she thought. I don't want to hear it. I can't bear losing Crystal, too.

'Oh, sweetheart, she's going to be just fine. That should have been the first thing I said!'

Poppy heard her aunt's words, but she couldn't

process them quickly enough. Was Crystal really okay? She looked up, brushing away her tears with the back of her hand. Had she heard Sophie right? 'She is?'

'If you girls hadn't been down there and caught her, then maybe not. She could have gone down with colic in the night and...' Aunt Sophie didn't finish what she was saying. 'All that matters is that Mark has checked her and walked her, and if she needs meds in the night, he'll administer them. She's going to be fine, Poppy. I promise. But she did have a lot of oats all at once, so I know you're not going to stop worrying.'

Poppy threw her arms around her aunt's neck. 'I'm sorry. I'm so, so sorry.' She wanted her aunt to know how much it meant to her to be here, with Milly and Katie, and Crystal. And how sorry she was that trouble kept seeking them out.

'No, I'm the one who's sorry. I owe you all an apology for not taking you seriously and for not believing you. Jessica's mother was paying a lot of money for her to come here, but that doesn't mean I should have let her behave the way she did. I shouldn't have turned a blind eye to what was going on, and I should have known better than to let you take the blame for not caring properly for your ponies.'

'So what's going to happen then? To Jessica?' Poppy asked.

Aunt Sophie rubbed her forehead with the heel of her palm and flopped down on her back beside them all on the bed. Poppy wished they weren't doing so much to stress her out.

'Her mother was waiting for her in the car. She'd lied to her about forgetting something to get her to drive her here tonight, said she had a few last-minute things to do,' Aunt Sophie said while shaking her head. 'I told her mum what had happened, showed her the video, and she's already offered for Jessica to take over all of your chores. Plus, she said she'll be grounded indefinitely.' Sophie reached for Poppy's hand and Poppy squeezed her aunt's fingers tight. 'Her mother was horrified, although she didn't believe me until I showed her the video footage.'

'So Jessica will still be coming here?' Milly asked, eyes wide.

'Look, girls, the reality is that we need paying pupils like Jessica at Starlight. But what she did is inexcusable, and unless she genuinely makes amends for the serious things she's done to try to hurt you and your ponies, I'll have no other choice but to turn her away.'

'I kind of feel sorry for her,' Poppy admitted. 'I mean, you heard what she said down there, Mils. She doesn't even like horses. That's so sad.'

'She said that?' Katie asked, sounding shocked.

'Yeah, she said her mum makes her ride, and she doesn't even want to,' Milly confirmed.

Aunt Sophie looked surprised but she didn't say anything, just rose without a sound.

'Try to get some sleep, girls,' she said. She stopped at the door and flicked the switch to turn off the light, her smile warm as she looked back at them. 'We still have a gymkhana to go to in the morning, remember?'

When Sophie had closed the door behind her, Poppy looked at Milly then Katie. They'd caught Jessica, Crystal was going to be okay and tomorrow was the big day!

'I can't believe we're actually going to make it there tomorrow,' Poppy whispered to the others. She dived back under the doona with Katie and Milly, snuggling in so they could all fit again side by side.

'We're gonna kick butt tomorrow,' Milly said.

Poppy couldn't wipe the smile off her face and burst out laughing. She couldn't help it. Relief, excitement and nerves were all rushing around inside her, making her almost giddy.

'What's so funny?' Katie asked.

'Crystal isn't going to die, and we're going to the gymkhana tomorrow!' Poppy said.

Milly kicked off the covers and sat up. Poppy could see her wide grin in the fading light. 'I thought she was going to kill us. Sophie, I mean.'

Poppy nodded. 'Me too.'

'We need to stop causing Mrs D trouble,' Katie said. 'She looked pretty worried tonight, and losing a riding school pupil can't be easy.'

'She'll feel better when we win everything and make Starlight look awesome,' Milly said as she got up and went over to the window, looking down like she was trying to see the stables. Even though it was late, the moon was so bright that they could still see the shapes of the trees and the farm buildings.

'Do you think we'll be good enough?' Poppy asked.

'I don't think so, I know so,' Milly replied.

Poppy got out of bed and changed into her pyjamas, the moon casting just enough light through the window for her to see. The others followed her lead, then hopped into their own beds. Poppy sighed happily as she snuggled into her crisp, clean sheets.

'Do you think we'll ever be able to sleep?' Katie asked.

Poppy shrugged. 'Doubt it.'

She stared up at the ceiling. She didn't care about sleep. The important thing was that Crystal was okay, and Aunt Sophie knew the truth. That was all that mattered.

CHAPTER FOURTEEN

Gymkhana Day

Poppy opened her eyes and instantly sat bolt upright. It was gymkhana day! She quickly jumped out of bed.

'Wake up!' she yelled, laughing when Milly startled and glared at her, her hair all curly and dishevelled. 'Come on!'

Katie leapt up and Milly did, too. 'Not so loud,' Milly grumbled.

Poppy bent down to open her bag and pulled out her fresh pair of jodhpurs, pulling on socks before she stepped into the jods.

'No way! Look!' she squealed as she turned and saw what was sitting on the end of her bed; three brand new Yarraman River Pony Club shirts, ties and vests had been carefully laid out. 'We actually get to go in proper Pony Club uniform!'

'This is so cool,' Katie whispered.

Poppy picked up one set and watched as Katie hugged hers to her body. 'We're so lucky. I can't believe it.'

Poppy dressed as fast as she could. It was a proper Pony Club gymkhana, and that meant most of the other competitors would be in their Pony Club attire, so they'd fit in with all the others. Poppy pulled the tie on, relieved that it was a fake that she could just slip around her neck. *Phew!* She'd only ever seen her dad do his tie when he was in uniform, and it looked tricky.

Poppy was the first dressed, and she ran downstairs, hearing Milly and Katie follow as she headed into the kitchen. She quickly put some bread in the toaster and grinned at her friends, who were both dressed in the same outfit she was. As she wolfed down her vegemite toast, Poppy couldn't stop looking down at the purple vest – the tie the exact same colour but with tiny bolts of gold through it. She could hardly believe it!

'Let's go!' Poppy said when they'd all finished breakfast, heading straight for the door.

'Wait up!'

Poppy held the door when she heard Uncle Mark call out.

'Thank you for the new clothes!' she grinned at him. 'Are you coming with us?'

'No.' He frowned, but Poppy noticed he was holding his hands behind his back a bit awkwardly, like he was trying to hide something. 'I wish I was, but I have rounds to do. But I'll be home ready and waiting to hear all about it tonight.'

Poppy tried not to be disappointed. She would have loved him to be there at the gymkhana, cheering her on, watching her ride.

'What are you hiding behind your back?' Milly asked. Poppy rolled her eyes at her friend – she could never wait for anything.

Uncle Mark grinned. 'Nothing gets past you, mischief mouse.'

They all laughed, but Poppy's laughter choked in her throat as Mark passed them all brand new purple saddle blankets with gold piping around the edges. Poppy was lost for words.

'You girls are members of the club, and you need to look the part, right?' Mark said.

Poppy threw her arms around his neck, and she felt Milly and Katie pile on, too. 'You're the best,' she whispered into Mark's neck.

'Yeah, the best, Mr D!' Milly and Katie sang at the same time.

The three girls rushed off down to the stables, waving to Mark as they went, to give their horses breakfast. The brand new saddle blanket was soft against Poppy's hands as she carried it, and she couldn't stop rubbing her thumb over the rougher piping around the edges. It was so early that the sun wasn't up yet, and a cool breeze blew against her face as she walked fast.

Poppy wished Crystal was plaited like Cody and Joe, but it didn't matter. Nothing could take the shine off the way she was feeling right now. She couldn't wait to throw her arms around Crystal!

'What do you think Jessica's doing this morning?' Katie asked.

Poppy shrugged, not wanting to think about Jessica and ruin her happy thoughts. All she wanted to do was see Crystal.

'Thinking about how much she hates horses,' grumbled Milly.

'I wonder if–' Poppy stopped talking as she rounded the corner to the stables. She had to stop her mouth from hanging open. She was so shocked when she saw Crystal cross-tied outside her stable – she couldn't believe what she was seeing.

'What were you going to say...' Katie's voice trailed off. Poppy was vaguely aware of Katie and Milly next to her, and they were all three staring at Jessica who was stood on an overturned wooden crate next to Crystal.

'What are you doing?' Poppy whispered in shock. She didn't even approach Crystal, just stood staring.

'I promise I haven't done anything to hurt her,' Jessica said, eyes trained on Crystal's mane as she spoke. 'She's had some hay, and I brushed her down for you, and I'm trying to get her all replaited before you have to leave.'

Milly started to say something, but Poppy shook her head, not wanting Milly to give Jessica another telling off now that she was finally being nice. Poppy went to find an old feed bucket to stand on so she could help Jessica finish the plaits. She found one next to an empty stall and dragged it over, pulling it up next to Jessica. Poppy started on a lower section of mane that was still curly and in need of combing before replaiting. Poppy couldn't believe that she was about to stand alongside Jessica. She'd thought that nothing would ever make her forgive this girl for what she'd done over the last week, but now that Jessica was helping, it was hard to hate her so much – Crystal really did look beautiful.

Katie and Milly disappeared, and Poppy glanced at Jessica. There weren't many plaits left to do, and she was surprised all over again when Jessica looked back at her and gave her a small smile.

'Thanks,' Poppy said, finding the word hard to say. She wanted to thank Jessica for her help, but it felt a bit strange since it was Jessica's fault the plaits had to be redone in the first place.

Jessica stopped what she was doing. 'I'm really sorry, Poppy. I was so awful to you.'

'Yeah, you kind of were.'

'My mum finally listened to me about how much I hate riding, and said that we can sell Cleopatra. After she grounded me for the rest of my life.'

Poppy kept working, not wanting to look at Jessica. She couldn't understand why *anyone* would want to sell a pony like Cleopatra.

'She deserves to have an owner who loves her,' Poppy said, thinking about all the times she'd seen Jessica whip Crystal.

Jessica sighed. 'I know. I can see how much you all love your horses. And I totally get it if you hate me. What I did to Crystal, to Joe, was awful, I just...' Her voice trailed off, and Poppy turned to look at her, waiting for an explanation. 'I've always had someone to groom my horses and do everything, and so I didn't realise... It wasn't until Sophie explained to me exactly what could have happened to Joe that day, how badly he could have actually injured himself, and then the...'

'The fact you could have given my horse colic?' Poppy spluttered, interrupting her.

'I'm sorry. I know you love her and probably hate me. I shouldn't have done it.'

'Well, thanks for doing this anyway,' Poppy said, not wanting to talk about it anymore. 'Are you still coming to the gymkhana with us?'

'Yeah. Sophie even said that she might know

someone there today who'd be interested in Cleopatra, so I'll ride her and show everyone how good she is.'

Poppy secretly hoped she could beat Jessica, even though she did want someone nice to be impressed with Cleopatra and want to buy her. The horse deserved a good and horse-loving owner after Jessica.

'What time did you get here to do this?' Poppy asked, finding herself unable to hold a grudge against Jessica, even after everything she'd done. Crystal was looking even more beautiful than normal, with her mane all plaited like this, and Poppy found herself feeling almost grateful, as well as a little sorry for Jessica. Especially seeing as she was so hopeless that she didn't even understand the danger her actions could have led to.

'I got here pretty early, but it's okay.'

'I'll help you get ready if you want,' Poppy offered. 'Once we're done here.'

'Thanks,' Jessica said.

For the first time, Poppy could see that this girl wasn't so bad deep down. She understood that Jessica had been miserable, being forced to be around horses when she couldn't even stand the sight of them, and all she'd been trying to do was find a way to show her mum how much she hated it. Poppy knew that didn't excuse Jessica's actions, but she couldn't help thinking Jessica really shouldn't have been in charge of a horse if she didn't even know the basics.

'What would you be doing right now if you didn't have to be here?' Poppy wanted to know.

Jessica stopped what she was doing. 'All I've ever wanted to do is play tennis. I love it.'

'Do you think your mum will let you?'

'I hope so. Maybe when I'm thirty and not grounded anymore.'

Poppy stood holding Crystal, her friends on either side of her, and watched as Aunt Sophie loaded two of the riding school horses onto the truck.

'Your turn, Pops,' Aunt Sophie called out from the ramp.

Poppy made a clucking sound and Crystal happily followed her, going up the steep ramp and into the truck, where Poppy tied her on an angle beside one of the other horses. She double-checked the knot she'd made, then closed the partition so that Katie could load Cody.

Poppy passed Katie on the ramp, and noticed Jessica in her mum's Range Rover, with the float carrying Cleopatra behind it, ready to go. Poppy raised her hand and waved, still feeling weird about being nice to her.

Once Milly had finished loading Joe, Aunt Sophie put the ramp up and gestured for them all to climb up into the cab. Aunt Sophie had told them it would take half an hour to drive to the Yarraman River Pony Club grounds, and Poppy stared out the window, feeling butterflies in her tummy, while Sophie climbed into the driver's seat next to her and her friends piled in on the other side. They were all seated across the front of the big horse truck in a line, belted up and ready to go. Poppy wished she'd kept hold of her new saddle blanket instead of putting it in the gear compartment – she wanted to make sure it stayed beautiful. She was definitely going to take it home with her, so she could look at it all the time.

'So Jessica helped you get Crystal ready this

morning, huh?' Aunt Sophie asked.

'Yeah. She's not as nasty as I thought, I guess,' Poppy replied.

'You guess?' Milly scoffed. 'She just did that because her mum probably made her.'

Poppy wasn't so sure. 'I think she genuinely felt bad. She's so happy that she gets to give up riding. It's weird.'

'Yeah, weird,' Katie murmured.

Before they knew it they were pulling into the Pony Club driveway, heading through an open field where about ten other trucks and floats were already parked. Sophie stopped the truck, and the girls all jumped down to see a line of vehicles, all towing horses, making their way in, too.

Her tummy was all jumpy and squirmy as her nerves were making her feel all funny. But she was excited, too. She couldn't believe that she was actually about to ride in her first real Pony Club competition.

'Pops?' Aunt Sophie came up and put an arm around her. 'You ready for this?'

'Am I ever,' she murmured back, giving her aunt a quick hug with one arm as they stood side by side.

From where they were stood, Poppy could see different games all set up in the huge paddock. Poppy couldn't drag her eyes from it all. The bending poles, the barrels, the start and finish line for another game and then the show jumps set up in the one arena on the pony club grounds.

'Let's get these horses off-loaded and ready,' Aunt Sophie said, pulling Poppy back toward the truck.

Crystal was third in the truck, and Poppy turned her around and carefully walked her down the ramp after the first two were safely unloaded. She tied her to the side of the truck and opened up the door on the other side where all their gear was stored. The big truck was gorgeous, fairly new and sparkling white, with the logo of a black horse on the side. It was sign-written across one side by Aunt Sophie's main sponsor, one of the big horse feed companies. Poppy always felt so proud to be with Sophie, to have her as an aunty and her riding coach, because everyone knew who she was. Not many riders had the chance to learn with someone as amazing as Sophie, and Poppy had her as her aunt, too!

'Saddle up, girls,' Aunt Sophie instructed,

leading the riding school ponies and taking them around to the other side of the truck. 'I'm going to get these two ready, and then I want you warming up, ready for the bending race.'

Poppy ran her fingers over the gold piping of her new saddle blanket before lifting it up onto Crystal's back. The purple looked so pretty against her grey, almost-white coat.

'I can't stop smiling,' Katie said as she took her gear out.

Poppy had been in a little dream and had almost forgotten she wasn't there alone! 'Me neither. I can't believe we're actually here.'

'Ha ha, you'll believe it when I beat you!' Milly joked.

Poppy laughed with her friend before doing up Crystal's girth. As she reached for her bridle to put on Crystal, she felt a smile spread across her face. This was it. Her first gymkhana.

CHAPTER FIFTEEN

Competition Time

Poppy circled Crystal at the canter, settling her into an even rhythm. One, two, three, four. One, two, three, four, she repeated silently, chanting to herself just like Sophie had told her to. She was wearing her new gloves, and loved how soft the reins felt in her hands with them on, the way she could let the reins slip through her fingers so effortlessly when she wanted to.

Poppy was still chanting as they approached the first jump; they popped straight over. She was looking ahead to the next, eyes forward, looking straight through Crystal's forward-facing ears. The next jump was a simple upright with blue and white poles, and the one after had pretty little flowers in pots set up in front of it. But Poppy had learnt her lesson where distractions were concerned, and because she never bothered looking at them, neither did Crystal. They sailed around the course, taking the last jump fast before racing to the finish line.

The sound of applause burst Poppy's bubble of concentration, and she gave Crystal a big pat on the neck as she slowed to a trot, then a walk, and headed straight toward the arena exit and Aunt Sophie.

'You did great, Pops! Really great!'

Poppy was beaming, and her heart was racing she was so excited.

'There's someone over there pretty excited about seeing you.'

She looked across and saw Milly waving frantically, and she waved straight back at her with both hands, wondering what her friend was so excited about. Poppy urged Crystal on before realising she wasn't even holding the reins! Lucky Crystal's so well behaved and didn't take off!

'It's Tom!' Milly yelled out.

Poppy burst out laughing at Milly holding Tom in a playful headlock. Milly hadn't even met Tom before and she was acting like he was *her* little brother! Poppy quickly trotted Crystal over then jumped down, throwing her arms around him and pushing Milly out of the way. He was wearing his favourite Transformers T-shirt, grinning at her like he always did.

'You did really well, right?' Tom asked.

Poppy laughed. 'Yeah, we did great. This is Crystal. Isn't she gorgeous?'

'I guess,' Tom said, shrugging. She tickled his ribs to make him giggle, and he elbowed her out of the way. He always hated when she did that in front of anyone.

Poppy turned around to check who was riding next, but kept her arm looped around her brother. She didn't want to miss Katie's round. The rider before Katie had taken a couple of rails, then Katie was entering the ring, cantering in a circle before heading for the first jump. She knew it was mean, but Poppy was happy the other rider hadn't had a perfect round. It meant that either she or Katie had a better chance at winning! Milly was out of the competition because she'd taken two rails.

'That's Katie in the arena,' she told Tom. 'My other friend.'

Tom stood beside her and they watched Katie do a perfect round. The only difference between Poppy and Katie would be their time, Poppy knew, because they'd both gone clear. There were still a few other competitors left to go, including Jessica, so there could be a few of them yet who did clear rounds.

Poppy chatted with Milly as they watched Jessica ride, gasping when her horse stopped at the fence with the flowers in front of it.

'Poppy?'

Poppy spun around – the familiar, soft voice making her drop Crystal's reins. Her mum was standing behind her, arms open and a big smile on her face.

'Mum!' What was her mum doing here? She rushed into her arms and held on tight. 'I can't believe you're here!' Poppy breathed in and closed her eyes as she smelt the familiar, comforting smell of her mum's perfume on her clothes.

'From what I could tell you rode perfectly out there today,' her mum said into her hair.

Poppy let go of her mum just enough so she could look up at her. Her mum's big smile was like the mum she remembered from before her dad had died. It was like someone had turned the light back on inside of her.

'You actually saw me ride?' she asked, grinning.

Her mum squeezed her, arms still holding her tight. 'Of course I did. I'm so proud of you.'

'Mum, you haven't met Crystal!' Poppy suddenly burst out, letting go of her mum and picking up her fallen reins. 'Mum, this is Crystal. Crystal, this is my mum.'

Her mum laughed and reached out to stroke Crystal's neck. 'Pleased to meet you, Crystal. I've heard a lot about you.'

'I've heard a lot about you, too,' Milly said in a silly deep voice, obviously trying to sound like a horse, and making them all laugh.

Poppy rolled her eyes. 'Mum, this is Milly. You know, the crazy one I told you about.'

Milly pushed past Poppy, holding out her hand. 'Nice to meet you,' she said.

Poppy's mum hugged her instead of shaking hands. 'Now *you* I've heard a lot about. Poppy's had so much fun with you and Katie.'

'Hey, look over there, Mils,' Poppy said, suddenly

catching sight of Jessica.

Poppy felt sorry for Jessica when she saw her mum flapping her hands and arguing with her as she dismounted Cleopatra. They'd missed the rest of Jessica's round, but she guessed it had gone badly. She watched Aunt Sophie walk over and take Cleopatra's reins, leading the pony away and over to another girl that Poppy didn't recognise. She hoped it was the prospective buyer, because she had a big smile on her face, and when Cleopatra snuffed her hand it made the girl laugh and pat her.

Poppy leaned against Crystal, closing her eyes and basking in the sun as she turned her face skyward. Last night, everything had seemed terrible, and she'd been so scared for Crystal, but somehow everything had turned out just great. Her mum was here, Tom was here, and she still had more riding to do with some other games after lunch – all with her family there to cheer her on. The only thing that was missing was her dad, but she strongly believed he was up there somewhere looking down on her, seeing how well she was doing and how happy she was. How happy they all were.

'Oooh, are they announcing the winners of the

show jumping now?' Milly asked.

Poppy's eyes popped open, and she grabbed Milly's hand, dragging her over to where Aunt Sophie and Katie were standing, leading Crystal on her other side. 'I'll see you in a minute, Mum,' she called over her shoulder, not slowing down. She wanted to be with Katie as the winner was announced, and as the crackle came over the megaphone, a shiver of excitement ran down her spine.

'Fourth place goes to Katie Richards.'

'Woohoo!' Milly yelled.

Poppy clapped and giggled as she tried to whistle between her fingers like Uncle Mark had shown her, but all she ended up making was a feeble squeak with a lot of spit. She laughed at herself and gave up.

'Third place goes to Lexie Marshall.'

They all clapped, and Poppy watched as a girl with long brown hair in a plait walked forward to collect her ribbon. It was the same girl she'd seen meeting Cleopatra just before.

'It was a close contest for the first and second, but in second place we have…

Poppy held her breath, listening so hard, waiting

for the name. She'd done well, but... she gulped. Could it be her? Could she have done that well?

'Poppy Brown!'

Poppy stood stock still. *Second place*? She'd taken out second place!

'Poppy!'

Poppy could hear Milly saying her name excitedly next to her, then she felt a hard nudge in the ribs. 'Go!'

'I...' Poppy stuttered, looking over at Katie and then craning her neck to see if she could see her mum where she'd left her. Poppy waved and grinned when she saw her jumping up and down with Tom, clapping her hands. Poppy quickly passed Milly her reins and walked forward to the centre of the ring between the jumps to accept her ribbon, remembering to say thank you.

She ran back to Crystal, holding the silky satin red ribbon in her palm, and Aunt Sophie kissed the top of her head, taking the ribbon and tying it around Crystal's neck. Then her mum came from behind her and wrapped her arms around her. It was all a blur of people and words, like she was in a dream.

'Come on, let's get a photo of you and Crystal with your ribbon!' Aunt Sophie said. 'All of you, get in there!'

Poppy smiled and laughed, standing against Crystal as Aunt Sophie snapped photos. Katie appeared on one side of her, and Milly hugged her from the other. Over Milly's excited squeals, she could hear the click of Sophie's camera still taking pictures, and she knew she'd always look at those photos and remember this moment, celebrating with her friends and family. She'd come second in her first Pony Club competition. Second place!

As soon as Sophie put down her camera, Poppy grabbed her mum's hand and dragged her closer to Crystal, hugging her mum and her pony tight.

'You're the best horse in the world, Crystal. The best,' Poppy whispered.

And she meant it. Even if she had all the money in the world, she wouldn't buy fancy Cleopatra or any other pony. All she wanted was Crystal – which was perfect, because she already had her.

ABOUT THE AUTHOR

As a horse-crazy girl, Soraya dreamed of owning her own pony and riding every day. For years, pony books like *The Saddle Club* had to suffice, until the day she finally convinced her parents to buy her a horse. There were plenty of adventures on horseback throughout her childhood, and lots of stories scribbled in notebooks, which eventually became inspiration for Soraya's very own pony series. Soraya now lives with her husband and children on a small farm in her native New Zealand, surrounded by four-legged friends and still vividly recalling what it felt like to be 12 years old and head over heels in love with horses.

FEEDS AND NEEDS

Horses need a balanced diet, just like humans, to satisfy their body's needs. All horses need water, plus fats and carbohydrates for energy, protein for muscle development, vitamins and minerals for general health and wellbeing.

But not all horses are the same, which means they don't all need the same type of feed each day. How old a horse is and what it does – be it a sport horse or a work horse – affects its nutritional needs, and it is up to the owner to supply the right mix of feed for each individual horse.

Generally speaking, many horses will need only hay as extra roughage in their diet to help with digestion, and it's advisable to add chaff (chopped hay) to any grain feed and mix with water to make it easily digestible.

MILLY'S CHESTNUT PONY, JOE,
IS A FULL-HEIGHT PONY AT 14.2 HH.
HE IS THREE-QUARTER ARAB AND
ONE-QUARTER STOCK HORSE.

Crossbred horses like Joe, whose Arabian breed dominates his make-up, are a lot of fun to ride! Arabians are often very excitable, which is why they are commonly crossbred to make them calmer, and Joe's stock horse side helps to balance out his energetic nature. Because of his Arabian bloodlines, Joe has a beautiful natural movement, but he can be quite headstrong when he gets excited – just like his owner, Milly.

ACKNOWLEDGEMENTS

Penguin Random House would like to give special thanks to Isabella Carter, Emily Mitchell and India James Timms – the faces of Poppy, Milly and Katie on the book covers.

Special thanks must also go to Trish, Caroline, Ben and the team at Valley Park Riding School, Templestowe, Victoria, for their tremendous help in hosting the photoshoot for the covers at Valley Park, and, of course, to the four-legged stars: Alfie and Joe from Valley Park Riding School, and Carinda Park Vegas and his owner Annette Vellios.

Thank you, too, to Caitlin Maloney from Ragamuffin Pet Photography for taking the perfect shots that are the covers.